ZIA ERASES THE WORLD

ZIA ERASES THE WORLD

BREE BARTON

VIKING

VIKING

An imprint of Penguin Random House LLC, New York

First published in the United States of America by Viking,
an imprint of Penguin Random House LLC, 2022

Visit us online at penguinrandomhouse.com.

Library of Congress Cataloging-in-Publication Data is available.

Printed in the United States of America

ISBN 9780593350997

1 3 5 7 9 10 8 6 4 2

LSCH
Design by Opal Roengchai
Text set in Bohemia LT Std

For Mom,
who always has a Lightning Bug

Though my soul may set in darkness, it will rise in perfect light;

I have loved the stars too fondly to be fearful of the night.

—Sarah Williams

⊙

Every dictionary has secrets.

That's to be expected, seeing as how a secret is made of words.

Dictionaries are heavy things, whole histories packed onto pages thin as spun silk. They are keepers of light and darkness, shimmer and shadow. Each word a patchwork of ideas stitched by many hands over many years. String enough words together, and you can hold all we have ever seen or felt or suffered.

Is it any wonder that sometimes, with a dash of magic and a dollop of mischief, a dictionary may choose to lessen its burden?

A vanished pronunciation?

A dropped definition?

A missing word?

I know of one such dictionary. It lies in a half-forgotten attic beneath a silver sheen of cobwebs, waiting for a girl who knows what it means to hold a secret.

I know of one such girl.

z | ˈzē|

noun

1 the twenty-sixth and last letter of the English alphabet

2 denoting a third unknown or mysterious person or thing: *The dictionary was a family heirloom, passed down from* X *to* Y *to* Z.

3 the nickname of Zia Angelis, the hero of our twisty tale

On days I'm not brave enough to face the cafeteria, I eat lunch in the girls' restroom. It's not as bad as it sounds. You just sit on the floor, angle your body away from the toilet, and have all the napkins you could ever want in a soft, white roll.

Today I'm nibbling my marshmallow crème sandwich in the far stall when I hear voices.

My stomach seizes. I chose this restroom because it gets minimal traffic. I do *not* want people to know I'm a hopeless weirdling, unable to enjoy my lunch in the cafeteria with normal humans who sit in chairs.

"Just come over after school," says a familiar voice. "We can swim."

"Sasha has the most gorgeous pool," chimes in another.

Silently, I stand and peek through the crack, careful not to let my glasses clank noisily against the stall door. Who are they talking to? I only see two girls checking their reflections in the bathroom mirror: Sasha fixing her Afro puffy twists, and Jay squinting disapprovingly at her thick blond eyebrows. I know these faces well. They're my best friends.

At least, they used to be.

Last year I sat with Sasha Davis and Jay Peterson every day at lunch. We played this game where we'd make up stories about which teachers were secretly in love, then see who could invent the most ridiculous ship names to crack each other up. I was good at it. Like, really good. Once I made Jay laugh so hard she snorted raspberry limeade up her nose.

Then the Shadoom came out of nowhere, and I wasn't laughing anymore.

"You can spend the night," Sasha says to the mystery person. "If your parents are cool with it."

"I can't," says a third voice. "My mom's a week past her due date. She needs me home."

My heart squeezes three beats into two.

The mystery person is Alice.

Alice Phan is the new girl in sixth grade. I heard she went to private school before coming to Ryden. She wears cool bomber jackets with colorful sewn-on patches and three hair bands that never leave her wrist: gray, red, violet.

Last week in gym class, we were playing dodgeball when school villain Thom Strong chucked a ball at a girl's face and made her nose bleed. "Look!" he shouted. "Weirdo bleeds red!" Alice marched right up to Thom and told him he was an asinine bully. Usually I'm crackerjack with words, but even I had to look up *asinine* on Mom's laptop later. I thought it was an excellent choice.

"I just figured you'd want to hang out," Sasha says, "since you're new and all."

Alice buffs the bathroom tile with the toe of her combat boot. "Sure. Thanks."

"Maybe once your mom has the baby?" Jay offers.

"It's whatever," says Sasha. But I can tell she's half-hurt, half-annoyed. "See you."

Her red high-tops squeak as she walks out of the restroom, Jay's jeweled sandals tripping along behind.

Alice leans over a sink and exhales so much air I realize she's been holding her breath. She runs a hand through her chin-length black hair. It's hard to tell through the crack, but in the mirror her sharp eyes look shinier than normal.

"I see you," she says. "There under the stall."

Now *I'm* not breathing. Alice Phan is talking to me. Sure, we've said *hey* and *hi*. One time I tried an enthusiastic *howdy!* (mortifying). But a real, multi-word conversation? Not a chance.

This is one of those moments that make or break you, the kind you read about in books.

I take a big sip of courageous air.

"No you don't," I say.

"I really do."

"It's your imagination speaking. You're having a conversation with yourself."

"Are you going to open the door?"

It's no use hiding. My hand shakes as I reach for the silver handle from the inside. She reaches from the outside at the same moment. The door swings fiercely open.

"Hi," she says.

"Hi."

She nods toward my lunch. "I didn't know my imagination brown-bagged it."

"Even imaginations must be fed."

Alice cocks her head, the hint of a smile perched on her lips. "It's Zia, right?"

I nod, stunned—and pleased—she knows my name. I'm good at making people laugh, but only when I know them already. I'm not the kind of person who stands out in a crowd. Medium height, medium build, medium-fair skin, medium-brown eyes. I used to say I'm a "happy medium" sort of person. These days, only half of that is true.

"You can call me Z," I say, a little too quickly. "Like the last letter in the alphabet. I mean, obviously it's the last letter! Number twenty-six. Actually I'm half Greek, and the Greek alphabet has twenty-*four* letters . . ." I need to stop talking.

"Twenty-four seems reasonable," she says. "I'm Vietnamese, and our alphabet has twenty-nine letters, but six different tones. Mind if I sit with you, Z?"

"It's a bathroom."

"Yes, I gathered that." Alice gestures toward the cafeteria. "I don't think I have the strength to go back into the wild today."

I understand perfectly and usher her into the stall.

It's a tight fit, but we make it work. For maybe a whole

minute we sit in silence, two sphinxes guarding either side of the toilet. I offer her half my marshmallow sandwich, and she says no. I offer her my pink apple, and she says yes. There's a yellow bruise on the skin, but she eats carefully around it, then tips open the silver box for tampons and drops the core inside.

"You must think I'm weird," I say, right as she says, "This is cool."

She scrunches her nose. "What's wrong with weird? I'd rather be a weirdling than boring."

I feel a goopy gush of delight. Weirdling is *my* word, and somehow Alice knows it.

Shyly, I take off my glasses and use my sleeve to polish the rims. When the dark rims are shiny, it makes the tiny yellow suns pop.

Alice sighs and rests the back of her head against the stall door.

"Tell me something you want, Zia. And not, like, suede boots or a mocha cappuccino. If you were granted one wish, what would it be?"

My mind scrolls through the things I *should* say. From the big—ending world hunger—all the way down to trading in my Grizzy brown hair. That's a mix of *Greek* and *frizzy*, two things you never want your hair to be.

But I don't say hair or hunger. What I say is, "To get rid of the Shadoom."

A sudden gust of air shivers up my spine, tickling the tiny

follicles at the back of my neck. Maybe it's the bathroom vent. Or maybe it's the fact that Alice is a stranger, and I've never said that word out loud to anyone. Not to Jay. Not to Sasha. Not even to Mom.

The Shadoom is what I call the room of shadows inside me. I couldn't find a real word to describe it, so I had to make one up. That's not quite what the Shadoom *is*, but it's how it *feels*. No windows, no sunlight, no doors—just a dark hole in the scoop of my chest. It's impossible to explain and confusing to think about. How can an empty room be so full of fear and hurt and sadness? And if there's no light, what's casting all the shadows?

"The Shadoom," Alice echoes, thoughtful. When I realize she's not going to ask me to define my made-up word, I want to hug her. But I don't.

She snaps the three elastic hair bands on her wrist, then waves her hand around the stall.

"This place is cool because it's a secret. A secret suits you. Though you have to admit, it does kind of smell like—"

"Marshmallows," I finish. "Definitely marshmallows."

She gives me the side-eye, and we laugh at the exact same time.

yiayia |ˈyä-yä|

noun

1 the Greek word for *grandmother*, the mother of one's mother

2 a term of endearment for a cantankerous old lady with white hair and an Attifact full of secrets: *The day Yiayia arrived was the day everything went wrong.*

Mom is late picking me up again. I wait at our special spot—the far corner of the soccer field, so she doesn't get stuck in what she calls the Slow Drip of Parents. In other words: the carpool line.

Mom waits tables at The Sweet Potato in the afternoons and teaches dance in the mornings. She says the classes are silly, more like aerobics, with wealthy ladies in pink yoga pants gushing about "living in abundance." Mom used to be an amazing dancer—I've seen an old picture of her in her ruby leotard, and she looks like a shiny red streamer—but she says you can't do something for fun once you've started doing it for money.

I try not to get annoyed when her lunch shift at The Sweet Potato runs late. Mom gave up her dinner shifts so she could be home after dark, even though the tips were better. The Shadoom is always worse at night.

I'm on the lookout for our car, the crumbling old station wagon we call the Brownie. So when the U-Haul truck pulls up at the corner, I assume it's some other parent, a fellow fugitive of the Slow Drip.

Then the window rolls down.

"Hey, Z!" Mom calls. "Check out our fancy new wheels!"

I blink. Then blink again.

"Do you like it?" she says. "I-Haul, You-Haul, we all haul for U-Haul!"

Mom is trying to sound chipper, but her forehead creases the way it does when she's stressed. Her thick black hair is swept up into a ponytail with little wispies falling around her face. Mom is proof that not *all* Greek hair is out of control, as long as it's wavy. Give me Gravy over Grizzy any day.

"Why are you in a U-Haul?" I say. "Are we moving?"

"No, no, no. We're staying put. But your yiayia . . ." She trails off.

Yiayia is my grumpy Greek grandmother. She's like a piece of ancient pita bread: crusty, brittle, and not very sweet.

"Is this about the tests?" Last week Mom told me the doctors have been running a bunch of tests on Yiayia, and she's not exactly getting As.

"Yes. Sort of." Mom sighs. "Climb in, Sunshine Girl. I'll explain everything."

I swing myself up into the U-Haul, readjusting my glasses as I slide over the scratchy seat.

Mom has called me the Sunshine Girl for as long as I can remember. "Even when we're apart," she says, "you are the sunbeam in my life." When I was little, that was true. Poke me with a pin, and sunbeams would leak onto my sock.

But when the Shadoom came, it's like someone flipped a switch inside me and everything went from light to dark. Mom knows something is wrong, she just doesn't know how *big* a something. Partly it's that I haven't found the right words. Partly it's that I'm afraid to tell her. These days Mom is always stressed or tired, or stressed *and* tired. Her back and feet hurt from working all the time. If I tell her about the room of shadows, I can't be her Sunshine Girl, and right now Mom needs sunshine more than ever.

So I don't tell her what I said to Alice in the girls' restroom. I slap on a smile and crank up the sun.

"I'm just going to come right out and say it," Mom says. "Yiayia is moving in with us."

I choke on my tongue.

"What? Why?"

"Just for a little while," she says, in a way that makes me think it'll probably be forever.

"What about her house?"

"The doctors say it isn't safe for her to be there alone anymore. The stairs alone are an accident waiting to happen. So the house will stay empty for a while, until we figure out what we want to do."

"Where's she going to sleep?" I ask, even though I already know the answer. Mom and I live in a 1-1 apartment (one bedroom, one bath) because the 2-2s were too pricey. I actually don't mind sharing a bedroom. It helps me sleep knowing Mom is nearby.

"She'll take my bed," Mom says, just like I knew she would. "I'll sleep on the couch."

Dread washes over me. Losing Mom as a roommate is the actual worst.

"My sweet Sunshine Girl." She reaches across the seat and squeezes my knee. "How about a Lightning Bug?"

Mom and I have a secret code word, like in a spy movie. When I say *Lightning Bug*, she knows to tell me funny stories from the restaurant or do an impersonation of the wealthy ladies in pink yoga pants or hug me and tell me she loves me.

I'd never ask for a Bug around kids my age. Might as well eat some crayons and go back to preschool. But at home, when it's just Mom and me and the Shadoom tapping at my chest?

"Yes, please."

"So today at The Sweet Potato," she says, "I dropped a whole beverage tray on a sweet elderly couple. Two coffees and two ice waters. Hot *and* cold. Even lost the ramekin of mustard! It flipped over and dropped right into the hem of this gentleman's nice khaki pants. *Ploop!*"

I laugh. Mom is always dropping something on someone or uncorking a bottle of wine with dramatic flair and spritzing people. The customers love her anyway. Though she worries that her managers lose patience with her every time they have to give a customer a free bottle of wine.

A thought startles me. Does Mom lose patience with me

every time she has to give me a Lightning Bug? And another thing: if you lose enough patience, do you stop being able to find it?

My laughter lodges in my throat like a tiny green grape.

"I wish I knew what was scaring you, Z," she says softly, more to herself than to me.

I wish I knew, too. I want so much to tell Mom about the Shadoom, to find a better word for what's happening inside me, one that will make her understand. I've always loved naming things. Like the time Jay got a potbelly pig for her tenth birthday, and I suggested she name him Hamlet. Sasha and I thought it was hilarious.

Jay did not.

Names help make something ours. We name pets when they become members of the family. We name feelings because it helps us own them. And if the name you want doesn't exist? Make it up. Stitch two real words together or pluck a new one out of thin air. I invent words all the time. It's kind of my superpower.

Thanks to the Shadoom, my superpower seems to be offline.

"It'll all be okay, Sunshine Girl," Mom says, steering the U-Haul into our apartment parking lot. "I love you to the stars and back."

I smile, because I want so much to be the Sunshine Girl for

Mom. But sometimes the Shadoom feels as big as the world, if not the universe. Like it might swallow me whole.

What if the Shadoom is a giant black hole that gobbles up Mom's love star by star? What if I'm too big of a burden? Mom is dealing with enough already—working two jobs, paying the bills, and now taking care of Yiayia. She doesn't need a broken kid, too.

If I fix myself, Mom won't have to. I've looked and looked for a real word—a *dictionary* word—to help me understand what's happening inside me. I keep thinking that if I name it, I can claim it, and if I claim it, I can figure out how to make it leave.

The thing is, it doesn't matter if I have the right word to describe it. I don't know the true name of the Shadoom.

But the Shadoom knows mine.

xenium |ˈzēnēəm|
noun

ɪ a gift from a guest or stranger: *Is it still a xenium if you gift it to yourself?*

From Greek *xenos*, "stranger, guest." In ancient Greece, the most famous xenium was the Trojan horse, a gift that was not what it seemed. Today a Trojan horse is any present that looks innocent but might actually destroy you. Not recommended for birthday gifts.

In the beginning, my grandmother was nice.

Not let-me-bake-you-chocolate-chip-cookies nice, but not baklava brittle. Mom took me to stay with Yiayia whenever she couldn't bring me with her to work.

Yiayia lived in a wonderful witchy house straight out of a storybook, the kind where you just *know* a nightgowned ghost is lurking behind an upstairs window. There were creepy doll clothes framed under glass, two mysterious locked rooms I wasn't allowed in, and a giant spiral staircase curling up to the second floor.

I loved the staircase because of the pictures. There were dozens of them on the wall, some from Greece, some from after Yiayia came to America. She never talked about them—they were just there. I always lingered at the square photograph of a man with kind eyes and a bushy black mustache. "Your pappoúlis," Mom told me. "Your grandfather. He died before you were born." The words came out heavy, and I knew not to ask for more.

But my favorite pictures were the ones of Mom. Yiayia had roughly one billion, maybe because my mom was an only child like me. They were arranged on the wall chronologically, which meant I could watch Mom grow up as I climbed the stairs: Mom as a toothless baby on the bottom step, then a toddler with two front teeth on the second, then a big toothy grin on the third, then two front teeth missing again on the fourth. And on it went.

That's where I first saw Mom dancing in her ruby leotard. Right before she had me.

There were pictures of baby me, too, though not as many. I could see why Mom called me the Sunshine Girl. I was such a happy little chonk.

One day when I was visiting Yiayia, as fat drops of rain pelted the stained glass skylight that turned her living room into a kind of cathedral, she held out her hand.

"Come, come, Zioula mou," she said. *My little Zia.* "Éla. You are ready to see."

She led me upstairs and down a long, narrow corridor, where she stopped abruptly. A white string dangled from the ceiling. She grabbed hold of it and pulled.

I gasped. A trapdoor had opened like a mouth, with a dusty ladder for a tongue.

"You must not be afraid," Yiayia said, unfolding the ladder. "This is only my attic of artifacts."

"Your Attifact," I said. Even when I was little I loved mashing two words together to make a new word, like mashing two short men into a tall one. A *portmanteau*, the dictionary calls it. I prefer *shortmanteau*.

"Yes," Yiayia said, nodding. "An Attifact full with the old Greek relics, like me."

The Attifact was magnificent. A million boxes tumbled

onto cobwebby shelves stacked high with ancient books, glittering antique jewelry, and the colorful trinkets Yiayia had collected over the years. She showed me a locket that had once belonged to her childhood best friend. Pictures of distant aunts and uncles with Grizzy hair like mine. A charcoal drawing of Tzatziki, the family dog.

The same grandmother who had always snapped at me when I touched the glass figurines downstairs now let me hold all sorts of precious odds and ends.

"In the many odds," she said, "I have the many memories."

Until that day, Yiayia had never talked about her past. She looked years younger—and far less grumpy—sitting on the floor, remembering. I knelt on the creaky floorboards, taking in her stories like an attic mouse nibbling chunks of feta.

The books called to me, as books always did. I crouched beside the shelves, running my fingers greedily down their cracked spines.

"Where did you get all these books?"

"Some gifts, they are given to us," Yiayia said solemnly. "Some gifts we must take."

I had no idea what that meant. I turned to ask her, then stopped short.

At the far end of the Attifact, hundreds of bright blue eyes stared back at me. Unblinking.

"My matákia," Yiayia explained. "The matáki charm protect against mátiasma. The evil eye."

When I drew closer, I saw they were glass charms painted to look like eyes. But instead of three rings of color, they had four: electric blue on the outside, then pale blue, then white, then a black pupil dot in the center. Each pendant swung from a thin silver chain.

"Mátiasma brings bad luck," my grandmother said. "Can be small bad or big. Maybe you have headache. Maybe you lose husband in car accident."

I was six. I didn't have a husband—or, for that matter, a car.

"So you wear evil eyes to save you from the evil eye?"

Yiayia cocked an eyebrow, like she didn't appreciate being questioned. "What is this saying you have in English? *Fighting the fire with fire.* In our family, we fight many years."

I fixed my brown eyes on the matáki blue eyes, trying to see the Attifact from their point of view. How many family heirlooms were they watching over? How many secrets were buried in these boxes, waiting for me to unearth them?

From that day on, I begged to go to the Attifact on every visit. It felt exciting and a little bit dangerous. I was fearless back then.

But my grandmother never told me stories like she had the first day. Almost as if she used them all up that rainy afternoon. And she didn't talk about my pappoúli, not once. I still remember the day his mustachioed picture disappeared from the staircase wall. I wondered if my grandfather was keeping Tzatziki company in the attic, but I couldn't find him there.

Over the years, Yiayia grew less and less inclined to pull down the trapdoor. Sometimes she complained her knees ached. Sometimes she muttered in Greek. Sometimes she grew very quiet, a far-off look in her eyes.

"I am too old, Zioula mou," she'd say.

And then one day, everything came to an end.

⊙

I was ten. Plenty old enough to go to the Attifact alone, even though Yiayia had strictly forbidden it. That morning she was snoozing in her purple paisley rocking chair, snoring lightly. Her snores always gave me the impression there was a kitten stuck in her nose.

Silently, I crept upstairs, unlatched the trapdoor, and scaled the ladder.

The first thing I noticed was the absence of things. Most of the shelves were empty. No trinkets, no photographs, no odds. I felt a grip of sadness. Why were so many artifacts missing? Had Yiayia gotten rid of them?

A flash of gold caught my eye.

One book had survived the purge.

It was half-hidden underneath an empty box. A gigantic tome, faded blue with gold-rimmed pages. It must've been at least a hundred years old. In all my trips to the Attifact, I'd never seen it.

I blew off the dust and read the curly golden words on the cover:

C. SCURO

DICTIONARY

13TH EDITION

My fingertips traced the half-moon notches on the side: A, B, C. Thumb cuts, they're called. A librarian taught me that. I'd only ever held a paper-and-ink dictionary in the school library. Mom's laptop ruled supreme at home.

Why hadn't Yiayia shown me this dictionary? She knew how much I loved words.

Something crunched under my shoe. I lifted my foot and saw a cracked blue orb.

As I stooped to cup the broken matáki, Yiayia started shouting from downstairs. An angry stream of Greek smashed up the ladder, pinning me in place.

I clutched the charm tighter—and felt my fingernails dig into my palm.

My hand was empty.

Had I dropped it? I didn't have time to look, because Yiayia's head poked up from the trapdoor, her face flaming red against her white hair. She looked like a furious peppermint.

I started to apologize, but she wouldn't hear it. She marched me downstairs and called Mom. I was scared. I'd never seen Yiayia like that.

But that wasn't the only reason.

I hadn't dropped the matáki. One moment it was in my palm, the next it was gone.

Or was it? The more I thought about it, the more I doubted myself. What I'd felt couldn't be real. If I told anyone else, they'd think there was something wrong with me.

Later that night, when I tried to explain to Mom, she shook her head.

"I should never have left you there." There was something hard in her voice I hadn't expected. "You're old enough to stay home by yourself now."

She meant it, too. I haven't seen Yiayia in over a year.

I still get the shivers when I remember the coolness of the matáki charm against my skin. The way my palm seemed to shimmer a dusky blue, then white, then black, until finally the dust vanished, too.

weirsh |ˈwirsh|
verb

1 to make a weird wish: *Why wish upon a star when you could weirsh upon a dictionary?*

From Middle English *wyrd*, "having the power to control destiny," and Old English *wýscan*, "to want something impossible."

A bunch of dusty furniture is jammed into our apartment when Mom and I get home. Bookshelves, chairs, a coffee table with yellowing copies of a Greek women's magazine pressed under the glass, and a tall grandfather clock.

Make that a grand*mother* clock.

"Éla, Zioula?" Yiayia's voice sounds small and echoey. "Where are you?"

"Where are *you*?" I answer. I can't see her amid all the clutter.

Mouseimus, my fat tabby cat, jumps onto the coffee table. Full name: Gluteus Mouseimus. My crowning achievement.

When he rolls over, offering his belly to be scratched, I hesitate. Sometimes when I pet Mouseimus, it stirs up memories of the movie I watched the night the Shadoom arrived, a movie where a mama cat doesn't come home. Mr. Mousie's white tummy is so soft and vulnerable that I think about what it would be like to lose him—or worse, Mom. In that moment, I get a taste of how it feels to be truly, terribly, foreverly alone.

I scoop Mouseimus up like a baby doll instead. He meows like a babycat.

"Zioula mou!" Yiayia's voice claws its way out from the jumble of furniture. I don't know why she sounds so angry. It's not like I can pole-vault over the mess. "I am here!"

I find her tucked into the purple paisley rocking chair she's had since forever. Only it can't be her, because she looks nothing like the Yiayia I remember.

Her hair, usually a white cumulus poof, is mashed against her scalp. I've never seen her without her bright pink lipstick or big, bold jewelry. But now her face and neck are bare. Without her makeup, I see her eight jillion age spots. It's like a bottle of Worcestershire sauce exploded on her head.

The last time I saw my grandmother, she was spitting mad. But even Angry Peppermint Yiayia would be better than this.

I take off my glasses, squinting to see if I can change her back into her original shape.

"Éla! Come, come!" she cries. "How many tears since you give your yiayia a bliss?"

"She means years," Mom says. "Not tears. And I think bliss means kiss. She's just a little confused."

I restore my glasses to their rightful place, then stoop to give Yiayia a peck on the top of her head. It's like kissing holiday tinsel.

"I have missed you," she says, and there are no claws in her voice anymore. "My little Zioula girl."

Suddenly she shoots out a hand and grabs my arm, startling me. "Did you remember to take away the kittens? The mountain lions, they are eating hungry. They come in the night."

"It's okay, Mana," Mom says quietly. *Mana* is Greek for *mom*. "You can let go now."

Yiayia releases her grip on my arm, hand trembling. "If you would only take this. The lions come down from the mountains, they are *ravenous*."

Mom chews her lips, face dunked in worry. She's looking at me, but her eyes are far away. She isn't here, and Yiayia isn't here—their bodies are still in the living room, but their brains went somewhere else. Fear dribbles cold down my spine.

"The mountain lions," Yiayia murmurs. "If you would only listen."

There are no mountains for a thousand miles.

⊙

My bedroom is unrecognizable.

It looks like ancient ruins, only instead of crumbling statues there are towers of old-lady clothes and boxes bursting at the seams. I wander through the wreckage, feeling the same magnetic pull I always felt at Yiayia's house, the invisible thread drawing me to the Attifact. A strange sensation, since the Attifact isn't here.

Or is it?

A suitcase yawns open on Mom's bed—now Yiayia's bed, I guess. My fingers itch as I step closer and shove a slippery mound of nightgowns aside. A thrill spins through me when my knuckles scrape against something hard.

The C. Scuro Dictionary: 13th Edition.

It's exactly how I remember: blue and dusty and ancient, infinitely better than Mom's boring laptop dictionary. I lift the book from the suitcase and run my finger down the silky golden edges. The pages catch the light.

Carefully, I lay the dictionary on the bed. It's massive, thicker than a loaf of bread and twice as wide. My thumb finds the z notch. I take a breath—and pry it open.

The words are tiny, so tiny, even more beautiful than I imagined. Font elegant and curly, black ink glimmering like it's wet. The two pages I'm poring over take me all the way from the letter z to ZERO, including five drawings for ZAMIA, ZAPHRENTIS, ZARF, ZEBRA, and ZEBU.

I know what exactly *one* of those words means. I bet Alice would know more. Frowning, I trace the z thumb cut. The letter z has the third-fewest words in the alphabet, the bronze medalist of the English language (x and y claimed gold and silver). Yet when I pinch the rest of the z pages between my fingers, they're more than an inch thick. I start to flip ahead, but something goes wrong, and instead the pages flutter backward, landing me solidly in Y. From YOU to YOURS.

"Z!" Mom shouts from the living room. "I could use your help!"

"Okay!" I shout back, annoyed.

I start to close the book, but my thumb gets snagged in M— and then I see something.

Cut into the pages is an eye.

Between MATADOR and MAT BOARD, someone has carved out a small eye-shaped hollow. Nested inside the hollow is a blue matáki.

My stomach jellies. If I touch this one, will it vanish, too?

Warily I scoop out the eye. It has the same four circles as the glass pendants—electric blue around pale blue around white around black—only this one is hardly larger than my thumbnail. More of a baby matáki, really. A babáki. And it's made of something much softer than glass.

I sniff it. The smell is instantly familiar.

An eraser.

"ZIA!" Mom yells.

With a sigh, I snug the babáki back in its hollow. Then I tuck the dictionary under my pillow. On second thought, I move it into my book bag. I'm sure my grandmother would give it to me if I asked anyway.

I flash back to something Yiayia said years ago. *Some gifts, they are given to us. Some gifts we must take.*

Who hides an eraser inside a dictionary?

vamoose |və-ˈmüs|
verb *[slang]*

1 to depart quickly, like a moose decamping in the forest: *If a group of moose vamooses, do they actually vameese?*

The C. *Scuro Dictionary* comes with me to school.

My backpack is ten times heavier, but it's worth it. While my science teacher, Mr. Brockmeier, demonstrates how to pin dead moths to a mat board, I reach surreptitiously into my bag. I'm getting better at flipping straight to the babáki. I love how my fingertips smell after I've touched it, that chemical rubber pinch.

At lunch I decide to be courageous. I'll find Alice, show her the dictionary, and strike up a real conversation. She digs words, too. It's the perfect plan.

But the moment I step inside the cafeteria, I know I've made a mistake. My sizzling courage evaporates like drops of water on a hot stove.

I see them at our old table. Sasha and Jay. The Mighty Zashay, we used to call ourselves. We weren't a clique, at least not a mean one. Since Sasha is a singer, sometimes Luis and Katlin and a few other choir and theater kids would eat lunch with us. After Jay joined the soccer team, her teammates came, too. We made jokes and tossed grapes into each other's mouths and traded Cheetos for Doritos.

I catch Sasha's eye. She stops midsentence, taco halfway to her mouth. Watching me.

And just like that, I'm back at her house. Sasha's twelfth-birthday-pool-party-sleepover-movie-night-extravaganza at the end of summer. Everyone having fun: laughing, swimming, eating burritos. Sasha's mom setting up a big screen for the outdoor movie. Sasha's dad poking little purple candles into the peach cobbler he made from scratch. Mr. Davis's homemade peach cobbler is Sasha's absolute favorite—and it used to be mine, too. Whenever she brought some to school, we'd all fight over it.

I hate that now every time I see a peach at the supermarket, I feel sick to my stomach.

I can't do it. Can't pretend to be normal. Not today.

Chin tucked to my chest, I shrink away from the cafeteria, Sasha's eyes searing a hole in the back of my braid.

⊙

In the girls' restroom, my sandwich tastes like sour marshmallows.

At least this time I've got something to read.

⊙

The C. *Scuro Dictionary* is over three thousand pages long.

It isn't all words and definitions. There are full-page illustrations of flags and butterflies and world maps. I find a periodic table of the elements, constellations and stars in both hemispheres, and pronunciation guides where strange little symbols transform even basic vowels into something exotic and unpronounceable.

Å Ę Ĭ Ō Ü

At the top corners of each page are two words in bold: the first and last words on that page. Some of the pairings crack me up.

WEALTHY ⊙ WEASEL

KINGDOM COME ⊙ KITCHEN SPONGE

POODLE ⊙ POOP

On a whim, I look up WEIRDLING. My jaw practically drops into the toilet.

weirdling |ˈwird-ling|
noun

A tiny weirdo.

The fact that WEIRDLING is in the dictionary is, well, weird. Then again, Alice used the word yesterday. Maybe I didn't make it up after all.

Someone jogs into the girls' restroom. My stomach clenches when she claims the stall next to mine. A little fart squeaks out, then a giggle. I don't breathe again until the toilet flushes and the giggly farter skips happily out of the restroom and into the rest of her day.

How nice that must be, using the bathroom as a bathroom. Not as a place to hide.

My breath catches at the thought. And suddenly there's one word I want to look up more than anything. I know it's impossible. It won't be there.

But what if it is?

My fingertips find the thumb cut for S. SAFE. SCHOOL. SERPENT. As the pages flutter past, I don't dare breathe.

There's a whisper of space between SHADOOF and SHADOW.

No Shadoom. No little black room.

My stomach plummets to the cold tile floor.

Gently, I close the dictionary. Slip it back into my bag, embarrassed. Of course I can't find the word I made up for the feeling I can't explain.

Did I really expect the C. *Scuro Dictionary* to fix everything?

☉

Ryden Junior High has an Olympic-sized pool, even though we are a far cry from Olympians. Some rich guy donated money for a big hole of chlorine water. Mom says the pool is a breeding ground for ear infections. I say it's a breeding ground for evil.

Every time we have swim gym in seventh period, it takes me back to Sasha's pool the night of her party. The pale blue water fading to midnight blue, so dark I couldn't see the bottom.

Honestly, even if the Shadoom *hadn't* come, sixth grade is hard enough without exposing your blazing white cheeks for the whole world to see.

Do my butt bones stick out? Are my boobs growing unevenly, like maybe one is pear-shaped and the other's a dried mango? What shape are boobs supposed to be? Will the other kids laugh at me?

There's so much to be afraid of, so many ways I might be made wrong.

Which is exactly why I put my swimsuit on at home under my clothes on the days we have swim gym. That way I never have to be naked in the locker room. The trick is to keep my clothes on until the last possible second. Once I'm sitting on the side of the pool with my feet dangling in the water, I strip off my T-shirt, then wriggle out of my shorts—yes, it's awkward—and chuck them onto the bleachers behind me.

That's always worked just fine . . . until today. Today I made an egregious mistake.

I don't even realize it, not until two girls start pointing and snickering. I look down and my face blisters with shame.

When I put on my swimsuit this morning, I must have been distracted. The bedroom was a disaster zone with all of

Yiayia's junk everywhere. So I guess I forgot to take off my underwear. Not just any underwear: the pink ones with dancing strawberries in top hats.

In other words: I'm wearing dancing strawberries in top hats *underneath* my swimsuit, which is nineteen different flavors of embarrassing.

Tears jab at my eyes like little pushpins. I want to run somewhere—anywhere—but it's too late. Thom Strong strides up to me in his camouflage trunks.

"Hey, Granny Panties. You know your underwear doesn't go under your swimsuit, right?"

Thom is much bigger than I am, with a bleached blond buzz cut and angry orange freckles. I stare straight ahead, hoping bullies are like dinosaurs: if you stay very still, they might not see you. Why is he doing this? Thom always swims in a long-sleeved T-shirt, and I don't tease *him* about it.

I fumble for my towel, muttering something along the lines of "I'm sorry." Of all the words in the English language, those are the only two I can find.

Thom laughs. "You said it, Panties. You *are* sorry."

He whoops loudly and cannonballs into the pool, leaving me drenched and shaking.

No matter how hard I try to be normal, I always fail.

Alice walks out of the locker room in a turquoise swimsuit with mermaid scales. It's the loudest, brightest suit I've ever seen, and she wears it without a trace of self-consciousness. We lock eyes. I look away, not wanting her to see the tears in mine.

Why would Alice Phan ever want to be my friend? She's the textbook definition of courageous. She's the new girl, yet somehow she's not afraid to take on Thom Strong. I am chicken noodle soup shaped like a human.

I turn and run to the locker room quicker than soup off a spoon.

unflappable |ən-ˈfla-pə-bəl

adjective

    1 showing calm in a crisis: *Alice is unflappable*.

    2 not easily flapped

The first thing I do is strip off my clothes and wad the dancing strawberries into a humiliated ball.

I hate the pool. Hate it hate it hate it. Just one more thing that went horribly wrong at the start of sixth grade.

Quickly I yank my swimsuit back on, terrified someone will see me naked. I hurl the sorry clump of underwear into my locker and slam the door. The metallic screech echoes through the empty room.

Then I reopen the locker, mutter a quick "I'm sorry" to my underwear, and un-clump it. This happens sometimes, me apologizing to inanimate objects. I figure it's not their fault I'm feeling whatever I'm feeling. They shouldn't have to suffer for it.

I fold the underwear, tuck it deep inside my backpack—and pull out the dictionary.

Maybe it's weird that an old dusty book of words gives me comfort. But words aren't mean. They don't make you feel small or broken. And if someone else does, you can look up SMALL and BROKEN in the dictionary and find them in permanent ink, proving someone else felt those things, too. Probably lots of someones. Who wouldn't be comforted by that?

I plop down on the bench and dig my finger into the P notch. The dictionary flops open. There, smack dab in the middle of the page, is a long rectangle with tiny waves.

POOL.

Huh. Flipped right to it. What are the odds?

pool |ˈpül|
noun

1 a puddle of standing liquid
2 a swimming pool
3 the school pool at Ryden Junior High: *A big hole of chlorine water that's a breeding ground for evil*

I slam the dictionary shut.
What?
Obviously, I read it wrong. I slap my forehead a few times, banging out the cobwebs. Rub my eyes vigorously. Then gulp some air and find the half-moon thumb cut for P.
Once again, the dictionary opens right to POOL.

3 the school pool at Ryden Junior High: *A big hole of chlorine water that's a breeding ground for evil*

I'm full-on shivering now. Possibly because they keep the AC in the locker room cranked to subarctic levels. Possibly because a hundred-year-old dictionary just referenced the pool at Ryden Junior High using my exact words.
Is this a prank? Did someone add that definition?
I rub the ink to see if it smears. It doesn't. If a kid broke into

the locker room and forged this entry, they did an excellent job: the font, size, and color are a perfect match.

My fingers twitch. If someone could add words to the *C. Scuro Dictionary* . . . does that mean someone could also erase them?

Once the idea plunges its hooks into my brain, it takes off. I could get rid of that last definition. What's the harm? At least then *I* wouldn't have to look at it. And I'd make my dictionary a little lighter, free of that bully-infested, over-chlorinated hole.

The baby matáki pops right out of its cave. The blue eyeball cuddles in my palm, like it finds me comforting, too. I pinch the eraser between my thumb and forefinger—it's smaller than it looks—and slowly, carefully drag it back and forth across the page.

The ink comes up easily. So it *is* erasable. I don't know why anyone would print a dictionary in erasable ink, but I'm rolling with it.

When I'm done, definition number three is gone, along with the eerily appropriate sentence. I feel a giddy sense of power. Goodbye, Ryden Junior High pool. Goodbye, breeding ground for evil. POOL only has two definitions now.

I snug the babáki back into the dictionary, lick my fingertip, and dab at the blue nubbins until the page is nice and clean. A blank white rectangle stares up at me.

Much better.

"Zia!"

My heart lurches toward the sound of my name. Alice strides into the locker room, wearing gym shorts and a cheddar-orange tank top that says GUARD YOUR CHEESIES. Somehow she changed out of her mermaid swimsuit without coming back to her locker. Impressive.

"Why'd you run out?" she says. "We were crushing it!"

"Crushing . . . what?"

She looks at me like I've sprouted a third elbow. "The match."

I picture jumping on a matchbook and crushing all the matches.

"Why are you in a swimsuit?" Alice shakes her head. "Never mind. Not important." She grabs my hand. "We need you out there, Z."

She leads me out of the locker room, back to the pool—and suddenly I'm stumbling, my heels sinking into a strange, soft substance. I stagger forward, kicking up bright yellow sand. Four of my classmates stand in a square formation, staring at me, and I stare back, trying to understand what's happening.

"Watch out!" Alice cries, but it's too late, I've gotten tangled in some kind of net, and I'm going down, down, down and taking the net with me, like a sad fish with arms.

"So much for volleyball," I hear a girl mutter.

And that's when I realize: I am stuck in a volleyball net. On an indoor volleyball court.

The pool is gone.

Thomas J. Strong |ˈtä-məs ˈjā ˈstrȯŋ|

proper noun

    1 an asinine sixth-grade bully: *Thomas J. Strong always wears long sleeves.*

In the end, they have to cut me out of the net with a pair of scissors from the front office.

I hardly notice. All I can think about is the pool. Or *lack* of pool.

One minute Thom was cannonballing into the water. The next I was tangoing with a volleyball net. Though *tangling* is probably more accurate.

"Love your swimsuit, honey," says Mrs. Nelson gently as she snip-snips with the scissors. Mrs. Nelson is my favorite of the school receptionists. She has always been nice to me. But now I can feel her watching me intently, like I've gone off the deep end. The metaphorical deep end, since the literal deep end no longer exists.

"Why don't you put your clothes back on while I call your mom?"

She gestures toward my bag, which someone must've brought from the locker room. Every muscle in my body clenches. Did they take the dictionary?

I thrust a hand inside. Relief whooshes through me. It's there, solid as ever. So are my glasses, tucked safely back in their case, and my T-shirt.

As I poke my arms through the sleeves, I try to make sense of what happened. Mrs. Nelson is calling Mom to come get me, because she thinks there's something wrong with me. Maybe she's right. But not for the reason she thinks.

I didn't just erase the Ryden Junior High pool from the dictionary.

I erased it from Ryden Junior High.

⊙

When Mom gets to the front office, she's still wearing her server apron from The Sweet Potato. Ever since the night of Sasha's party, seeing that orange apron feels like a warm, sugary lump of comfort.

Mom says hi to Mrs. Nelson, then gives me a hug.

"So," she says, pulling back and studying my face. I study hers. Is she mad? Disappointed? Has she finally figured out her daughter is a total weirdling?

She smiles. "How about some ice cream?"

I say yes, of course. I'm only human.

The question Mom *really* wants to ask doesn't come until we're almost at the ice cream shop. I can tell she's been chewing over how to phrase it ever since getting Mrs. Nelson's call.

"Are we going to talk about what happened at school?" she says, in her Keep-It-Casual voice.

I imagine the honest answer to that question. *I stole Yiayia's dictionary, which I guess is magic, and when you erase a*

word it disappears for real, so I ended up erasing the school pool.
Whoops.

"Did you have to leave The Sweet Potato early?" I say, using my Change-the-Subject voice.

"It was fine. Not much of a lunch rush today."

Thanks to Mom, I know a good bit of restaurant slang. *Lunch rush* is when they're slammed at lunchtime. *Eighty-six fries* means they're out of fries. *Bev nap* is when a customer drinks too many alcoholic beverages and falls asleep on a napkin.

Just kidding. It's a small square napkin that you have to shake salt on so it doesn't stick to the sweaty bottom of a glass.

"Does that mean you didn't get many tips?" I ask.

She grimaces. "Not as many as I'd like."

Mom doesn't love working at The Sweet Potato. Most days she worries about not making enough money or getting fired for dropping things. And lifting all those heavy trays makes her back hurt. I wish she had a job that didn't make her scared and sore all the time.

I don't want to add to Mom's stress. But I need to know the consequences of what I erased.

"I was wearing my swimsuit," I say carefully, "because I thought I'd be swimming in the pool."

She cocks her head. "The neighborhood pool? It's only open in the summer."

"Or maybe, like, a school pool," I say, using my No-Big-Deal voice.

"Since when has Ryden had a pool?" Mom frowns. "That's just asking for ear infections."

"So true." I nod fiercely, hoping she doesn't continue this line of questioning. "Who wants that?"

My brain is working overtime, slotting things into place.

Erasing the school pool didn't just erase the physical pool. It erased the whole *idea* of it.

The realization makes me dizzy. Not only did I get rid of the pool in the present, I wiped it clean from the past. For Mom, there was never a pool at all.

And it isn't just her. When I try to conjure up the school pool, the image is hazy. In theory I know my damp swimsuit is clumped inside my bag, proof that the pool did in fact exist. But it's getting harder to remember.

"Here we are," Mom says, pulling up to What's the Scoop? Usually the parking lot is crammed with oversized Rich Mom Cars, sugar-happy kids piling out to snag their after-school ice cream. But today the lot is eerily empty. Everyone's still at school.

"We don't have to get ice cream," I say, even though I could really use some. Mom and I only ever go to What's the Scoop? when we collect enough spare change from under the car seats and between the couch cushions, and we always split a single scoop.

"It's my treat," she says breezily. But the worry crease is creeping back, an apostrophe perched on the top of her nose.

⊙

"Hi, welcome!" chirps the girl behind the counter, whose nametag reads SCOOPERSTAR KATIE. "What's the scoop today?"

"Daughter's choice," Mom says. "Got any special flavors for us?"

"I'm so glad you asked!" Scooperstar Katie speaks only in exclamation marks. "The flavor of the day is Just Peachy!"

My stomach churns. I can't believe how little it takes to drag me back. Purple candles winking on the tray of cobbler Mr. Davis just pulled out of the oven. The smell of hot, bubbling peaches swamping the cool night air.

"We love peach!" Mom grins at Scooperstar Katie. "Would you be a peach and get us one scoop with two spoons?"

Guess Mom forgot all about *daughter's choice*.

But I don't say anything. I nod and say I like peach, too, because it makes Mom happy.

As Katie hacks the metal scoop into the bucket of Just Peachy, nausea swirls up my throat.

It's happening. I can feel it.

"You get first lick, Sunshine Girl." Mom hands me the ice cream. I stare into the cup. The sick feeling is congealing on my tongue, cold and chunky. I do not want to vomit on the floor of What's the Scoop? while Scooperstar Katie cries, "Here's a mop!"

"Be right back," I say.

I bolt toward the minuscule one-toilet bathroom, slamming the door behind me. Instantly the cheerful pink-and-white walls of What's the Scoop? vanish.

The room is pitch black.

"Just a bathroom," I say aloud, trying to be rational. "You love bathrooms, remember?"

Darkness slips under my skin.

I fumble desperately for the light switch. The overhead spits and flickers, then decides to stay on, bathing everything in a queasy green hue. I force my eyes to focus on harmless objects. Paper towels. Clorox spray. Seashell air freshener.

Nothing scary here, I tell myself. *I am safe in this bathroom.*

But I don't feel safe. My breath comes in painful, jagged bursts. I ease my bag off my shoulders, hoping this might alleviate the pressure in my chest. I press my back hard against the door.

It's no use. The Shadoom is here.

The shadows spread, spilling out of my chest and into the rest of me. They crawl through my blood. Bleed into my toes and fingers. Even my thoughts go murky. My heart constricts, squeezed in the Shadoom's dark fist.

I'm so ashamed. What kind of person can't even *look* at Just Peachy ice cream without having a total meltdown?

And there's another kind of shame, too. Shame for letting this happen. I should've walked out of the store the moment I heard the flavor of the day. But I don't know how to explain to

Mom why I can't eat peach ice cream or be alone at night or watch movies about cats.

She wouldn't understand the Shadoom. Even *I* don't understand it. Sort of like how, when Mr. Brockmeier explains the way an infection skulks through a person's immune system, I don't understand the science of it. But that doesn't make infections any less real.

I puff air out of my mouth. Slurp some back in. If I'm going to face this alone, then I need to be smarter about how to fight it. *Fighting the fire with fire*, as Yiayia would say. I may not know what the Shadoom is or why it comes, but I've gotten better at knowing *when* it comes. There are certain things that seem to trigger it.

A light bulb pops to life in the back of my brain.

I could erase those things.

No, no, no, says the voice in my head, the scrappy one that likes to pick fights with itself. *That would never work. That's like trying to get rid of fire by erasing sparks.*

Wouldn't erasing sparks erase fire, though? You can't have fire if you don't have a way to ignite the flame.

A strange new feeling is simmering in my chest. Ever since the Shadoom made its grand debut, I've felt helpless. I can't find the right word for it and can't make it stop. But having a magical dictionary?

That changes everything.

Every word is made up of other words. Definitions. Synonyms. Example sentences. Etymologies, which are basically superhero origin stories where the word is the superhero. If I break the Shadoom down into words that exist, maybe I can name the shadows. And if I name the shadows, maybe I can take them away, one by one.

Not only could I get rid of the Shadoom. I could make it so the Shadoom never existed.

I could be the Sunshine Girl again.

I'm already sinking to the floor beside my backpack, reaching for the zipper. My pulse thumps through my fingers. I paw past my swimsuit, which for half a second confuses me. Why do I have a swimsuit in my bag? The neighborhood pool is only open in the summer.

The school pool. Right. I shove my swimsuit aside—and realize my palms are clutching empty air. I stare at my hands.

What exactly was I holding? Some kind of suit?

A trill of excitement thrums down my spine.

This is exactly what I need.

I heave the *C. Scuro Dictionary: 13th Edition* onto my lap. Nothing drastic, I decide. Like Mr. Brockmeier says, every experiment should begin with a controlled set of variables. Keep it simple.

I'll start with PEACH.

sand |ˈsand|

noun

1 a loose granular substance resulting from the erosion of rocks

2 the sand in an hourglass or a grain of it; hence, a moment or interval of time

3 figuratively, a most unstable material, doomed to gradual destruction or diminution: *words written in the sand*

Outside the bathroom, Mom is standing at the counter, eating our single scoop.

"Sorry!" she says. "I had first lick. Okay, fine, maybe second and third licks, too. You've got to try this, Z. Might be the best flavor of the day yet."

I bait the hook. "Peach?"

"*Beach?* Never heard of that flavor." Mom laughs. "What's it taste like? Sand?"

The simmery-good feeling in my chest is bigger now, close to a roiling boil. When Mom offers me the cup, I take it. The ice cream inside is a dark and velvety purple.

Victorious, I dip my spoon. Flavor floods my mouth.

"Plum licorice!" shouts Scooperstar Katie, as if she can't keep the secret one second longer. "Don't you just love it!"

"Love licorice!" I shout back.

Actually, I hate licorice.

But I hate it a whole lot less than peach.

restaurant |ˈre-stə-ˈränt|
noun

1 a place where people pay to sit and eat meals that are cooked and served on the premises: *Sophia Angelis works at a restaurant to make ends meet.*

At home, I trip the light fantastic.

Meaning I literally trip on the cord of Yiayia's lamp and face-plant onto the couch.

"You okay, Z?" Mom asks, and I answer with a muffled but enthusiastic "yes!" I'm in too good a mood to be angry. As I wipe the couch smudge off my glasses, my brain is abuzz, compiling a list of all the words I'm going to erase.

"What are you doing, Mana?" Mom says sharply.

I look up to see Yiayia in the kitchen, shuffling after three silver mixing bowls as they roll across the linoleum. When the biggest bowl has settled, Mouseimus plops down inside it like a batch of chocolate cat cookie dough.

"Not sanitary," Yiayia grumbles. "I want make the spanakopita."

"We have a box in the freezer," Mom says.

Yiayia looks horrified. "I bake the *fresh* spanakopita, paidaki mou!"

Paidaki mou is a term of endearment that means "my little child," but it works particularly well when you want to scold someone. For us Greeks, affection and scolding seem to go hand in hand.

Mom sighs. "You're not supposed to be in the kitchen, remember? Too many ways to hurt yourself."

"I bake the spanakopita." Yiayia stares at the stovetop with her hands on hips. She frowns. "What is this?"

I blink. Does Yiayia really not know what a stove is?

Mom rubs her forehead crease, like she could massage it out of her skin. "You're proving my point, Mana. Please stay away from the stovetop. I don't want you to get burned."

Yiayia clucks. "You drown yourself in teaspoon of water!"

It's a funny expression in Greek—you use it when someone makes a big deal out of nothing—and I start to laugh. But Mom isn't laughing.

"You are not safe in the star, paidaki mou," Yiayia says out of nowhere. "All the stars on the road, too many."

"Do you mean cars?" Mom says. "I'm a very safe driver. You don't need to worry about me."

"What you mean, *cars*? You must so careful. So safe. If you would only take this."

A cloud passes over Mom's face.

"You look tired, Mana. Maybe it's time for an afternoon nap."

Yiayia grunts. "You break my nerves! I will nap myself." Chin lifted proudly, she shuffles down the hall.

Mom's shoulders sag. Barely noticeable, but I notice.

And then something changes in her face. She un-sags her shoulders and beams a smile in my direction.

"How about you, Sunshine Girl? After-school snack?"

"Sure! I love frozen spanakopita."

To tell the truth, I prefer Yiayia's spanakopita. But when Mom smiles, I'm cocooned in relief.

"I'll even microwave it for you," she says. "How's that for service?"

She stoops to pick up the mixing bowls, then gasps. *"Aggh."*

"What? What is it?"

Mom steadies herself on the counter, still bent over. "Just my back acting up again."

My own back twitches at the thought of her hurting. "Want some ice?"

"I want a different job," she groans, massaging her back. "Where I don't have to lift heavy trays all day."

There's a tickle at the back of my throat, an *aha!* waiting to be aha'd. Whenever Mom complains about work, I feel like I can't do anything to help her.

But now I can.

"I'm okay." Mom is standing straight again. "*You* okay? Do you need a Lightning Bug?"

For once I don't. All I want is to be alone with the dictionary.

"Maybe later. Lots of homework tonight. I should probably get started."

I hurry down the hall, Mom's voice trailing behind me.

"Let me know if you need help!"

Little does she know, I'm about to help her.

When I get to the bedroom, my grandmother is sitting on the bed, grumbling. I catch something about a mountain lion, followed by "grab an egg and shave it." This is clearly a Greek idiom I've never heard but will now be using as much as possible.

"Aren't you supposed to be napping, Yiayia?"

"Aren't you supposed to be freezing spanakopita?' she retorts, mimicking my exact inflections. It's strange how one minute Yiayia sounds like she's missing little pieces of her brain, and the next she's completely normal.

"Never mind," I mumble, scanning the messy bedroom. I need somewhere I can tuck myself away. My eyes come to rest on the closet.

Bingo.

I saunter nonchalantly across the room. The closet door is ajar, and I stand with arms akimbo, pretending to examine Mom's clothes. The minute Yiayia looks away, I dive in, tugging the door shut behind me.

Then I wait for the stars.

Last year, before I was afraid of small dark rooms, I spent a lot of time in this closet. I'd read, do homework, dream up new words. If I pushed the curtain of clothes aside, I could curl myself into the narrow strip of space behind Mom's dresses.

She even let me stick green glow-in-the-dark stars on the wall so I could find my way.

I mostly avoid the closet now, for obvious reasons.

But today, as the stars begin to glow, I am not afraid.

The C. *Scuro Dictionary* feels firm and reassuring as I shimmy it out of my bag. I pull my knees to my chest and balance the book on my bony kneecaps.

There, snailed in the closet, I ruminate. That's the sort of deep thinking the Persian poet Rumi did before he ate.

I could erase TRAY, but that seems like a wasted opportunity. Besides, even without trays, Mom would still be on her feet all day, hefting other heavy things at The Sweet Potato.

I could erase SWEET POTATO. In the hazy green light, I flip to the page with SWEETHEART ☉ SWELL SHARK at the top, where I learn that not only is a sweet potato an edible starchy tuber with sweet pink flesh—it's actually "the original potato." Who knew?

It feels wrong to erase the OP. What did sweet potatoes ever do to me? Even worse: What if I somehow erased *all* potatoes by mistake? I imagine a potato-less world, forever bereft of French fries, tater tots, and salty hash browns doused in ketchup.

My gut tells me it wouldn't work, anyway. Mom would still have to work at the restaurant, just with a new name. The Sour Grape. The Organic Carrot.

What if I erased RESTAURANT?

The idea lands in my chest with a pleasing little burp. Not gonna lie, though: I do like when Mom brings home food from The Sweet Potato, because—no offense, Mom—it tastes a lot better than the food she cooks. If I erase *all* restaurants, I might never eat a good meal again.

But if that means Mom has a different job that makes her less stressed, it's worth it. Right?

I hook the R thumb cut. It's only one notch back from s, so I'm surprised when the pages start flying by, flapping through my fingers like an ornery bird. They plop me down smack dab in the middle of J, where one word lords over the page with a whopping nineteen definitions.

I only make it through the first two.

job | ˈjäb|
noun

1 a paid position of regular employment
2 an odd or occasional piece of work: *Sophia Angelis works odd jobs to make ends meet.*

My throat tightens. There she is, right there in the dictionary. My mom.

Something thumps under my fingertips. A soft rubbery *thud.*

I give a start. Did the dictionary just *move*?

And somehow I know, without having to flip ahead a few

hundred pages, that the matáki eraser just jumped in its matáki hole. It's getting jittery. Anxious.

The C. *Scuro Dictionary* wants me to erase JOB.

I mull it over. If I got rid of JOB, Mom wouldn't have to go to work. But if she didn't go to work, she wouldn't make money, and then how would we pay for rent and food and mouse toys for Mouseimus?

Without a job, how would anyone pay for anything?

No, RESTAURANT is definitely the better choice. I flip to R— and the dictionary fights me. The pages feel more like sand than paper, slipping through my fingers. No matter how hard I try to wrestle them, I find myself back, once again, at JOB.

Fine. I'll consider it.

I squint at the other definitions in the dim light, just to see what I'd be getting myself into. I remember the school librarian saying every dictionary entry starts with a headword—in this case, JOB—and then all the related spin-off words are called the word family. Which is kind of sweet.

I catch on JOB with a capital J, meaning proper noun.

17 the Biblical patriarch who loses all he holds dear

18 one who sustains patiently a life of poverty and misfortune

19 masculine proper name: *That guy Job is really mad at his parents.*

Amen to that. What kind of parents would name their kid Job?

A chill sweeps through me. If I were to erase the whole word family, proper noun included, would all the people in the world named Job, like . . . die?

I shake the thought out of my head. I could just leave that definition, the way I left the other definitions of POOL. I could leave all of them, honestly, except the second.

2 an odd or occasional piece of work: *Sophia Angelis works odd jobs to make ends meet.*

I'm gripped by a terrible new thought. If I erase both the definition and the example sentence, and my mom is in the example . . . will it erase Mom, too?

Forgive the pun, but the thought is too horrible for words.

I bang the dictionary shut so fast it releases a cool swell of air, goose bumps prickling my skin. My heart is pounding.

This isn't as easy as I thought.

"Z?"

I jump, knocking one of the green stars off the wall.

"Zia?" Mom taps softly on the closet door. "You okay in there?"

"Yep!" I croak. It comes out more froggish than I intend it to. "Just thinking."

"Come eat your spanakopita," she says, "and we'll knock out some of that homework."

I stuff the dictionary into my backpack, relieved I don't have to decide anything.

Not yet.

quid pro whoa |kwid-‚prō-ˈwō|
noun

ɪ something that is given or taken in return for something else: *No gifts are given freely. There's always a quid pro whoa.*

From Latin *quid pro quo,* "something for something," and North American *whoa!,* "a command to slow down or reconsider, often used to express alarm, astonishment, or admiration of actor Keanu Reeves."

I'm back in the girls' restroom.

For once I'm not cowering in a stall. I just need to pee before first period. So I'm using the bathroom like a normal person when two girls come in, deep in conversation.

It's Sasha and Jay.

Of course it is. We never used this restroom when we were Zashay. Not once. Now apparently it's their toilette du choice.

I watch them through the crack, heart whumping in my chest. Sasha leans over the sink to inspect her reflection. Today her puffy twists are swooped into a loose bun.

"I saw what he packed me for lunch," she says. "I swear, if my dad makes me eat cobbler one more time, I'm disowning him."

I frown. Since when has Sasha hated her dad's peach cobbler?

"What flavor this time?" Jay asks. She, too, is wearing her hair in a bun. She pokes a few loose blond strands back into place. "Apple or cherry?"

"Ugh. Apple. The chunks get all soggy and gross."

My nose is smashed into the stall door so hard my glasses fog up. I try to breathe through my mouth instead.

"You want it?" Sasha says. "We can trade at lunch."

Jay wrinkles her nose. "No thanks."

Only then do I remember we're in an alternate universe where peaches don't exist. An alternate universe where instead of fighting over Mr. Davis's cobbler, I guess everyone thinks it's disgusting.

I feel a stab of regret. *Sorry, cobbler*.

But I also feel relieved. I won't ever have to see a . . .

Hmm. What was that fruit called again?

I squeeze my eyebrows together, trying to recall the shape and color. Round? Juicy? Orange?

Nope, pretty sure that's just an orange.

"Ugh," says Sasha, jolting me back. She narrows her eyes at the bathroom mirror, turning her face from side to side and lightly tracing her cheekbones. "I tried contouring this morning. Total disaster."

"I think your cheekbones look gorgeous!"

"Next time I'm going to watch a makeup tutorial."

"I'm sure your cheekbones will look gorgeous then, too."

Sasha rolls her eyes. I feel a little rush of friend memory. Jay has a habit of bombarding people with nonstop compliments to a degree that's almost worrisome. Sasha and I even staged an intervention once to make sure she knew she didn't need to constantly compliment us to be our friend. We called it the Complimention.

Now Jay laughs. "I'm doing it again, aren't I?"

"Yes." Sasha sighs. "Sorry, I'm moody. We have auditions for the musical today, so I stayed up all night rehearsing my solo, and I actually think it made me worse? I hate auditions. I freeze up every time. I know I'm good. But at auditions, I just . . . choke."

"Is there any way you can do a self-tape instead of a live audition? Where you film yourself singing? I heard that's a thing."

Sasha raises an eyebrow, impressed. "Look who's learning the lingo!"

"What can I say?" Jay shrugs. "I'm a jock who can google."

"Unfortunately I don't think they do self-tapes in sixth grade." Sasha sighs again, more dramatically. "I just wish Mrs. Harrison would give the parts to the people who deserve them."

"You would totally get the lead," Jay gushes. She smiles, catching herself.

Sasha smiles back.

I smile, too. Not that they can see me. But I tell myself that's okay. The thump of hurt in my chest is offset by a thump of happy.

I've got work to do.

⊙

AUDITION only has one definition.

audition |ô-ˈdi-shən|
noun

ɪ a trial performance to win a role as a singer, actor, dancer, or musician, consisting of a practical demonstration of the artist's talent: *Sasha hates auditions. She freezes up every time.*

I roll my eyes. So the dictionary's been eavesdropping on Sasha's private conversations.

Then again, so have I.

As I pry the babáki out of its pocket, I feel the same trickle of unease as I did about Mom. If Sasha is in the example sentence, and I erase the example, will it also erase Sasha?

Something shifts beneath my fingers.

Fresh black ink bubbles on the page.

I inhale sharply. *This* is new.

The ink moves quickly, curling and whirling, as the words beneath AUDITION rearrange themselves. Some letters disappear completely. Others lumber along, sprouting extra feet and hunched backs, round bellies and long necks. *S* twists itself into *W*, *a* stretches into *d*. It's so fluid, such an elegant dance, it takes my breath away.

I can't help but think the *C. Scuro Dictionary* is about to answer my question, even though I didn't ask it out loud.

Sure enough, when the words have settled, there is a new gleaming example.

Who doesn't hate auditions?

Well, there you go. I don't have to worry about erasing Sasha anymore.

I give the dictionary a friendly little pat.

"Thanks," I say, as the babáki kisses the page.

⊙

I am a girl reborn.

There are no words to describe how it feels erasing AUDITION for Sasha. I've always thought of a gift as something you give people. Not until today did I understand it can also be something you take away.

If I'm going to erase things for myself, why not do it for other people?

On the way to first period, I pass by the teachers' lounge and overhear my history teacher, Dr. Liu, saying how worried she is about her little boy who's home with a bad cough. I do an about-face and duck into the supply closet, where I scour the definitions of COUGH to see if any could potentially cause trouble. As I suspected, there's nothing but "hacking up phlegm."

Bye-bye, cough. As the Greeks say: sta tsakidia. Goodbye and good riddance.

In second period this guy Devon's face is all swollen because he stepped on a wasp nest, so I ask for a bathroom pass and go erase WASP.

In third period this girl Kathleen is complaining about how her mom keeps buying her ugly skorts and expecting her to wear them, so I ask for a bathroom pass and go erase SKORTS.

In fourth period my math teacher, Mr. Crumpton, assigns a worksheet on dividing fractions plus a new multiplication table plus a brain-crunching algebra problem, so I ask for a bathroom pass and go erase HOMEWORK. Because why not?

I ask for so many bathroom passes, my classmates probably think I have amebic dysentery.

Only one teacher gives me attitude. Crotchety Ol' Crumpton, of course. When he raises an eyebrow, I lean in and whisper, "This is a *closing punctuation* situation," and he hands me the pass so fast I get a laminated-paper cut.

I actually haven't started my period yet. But last year the girls' volleyball coach was fired after an insensitive period-shaming email went viral, so now all the teachers at Ryden are super careful.

It's not like I'm reckless. I check and recheck the entire word family before I erase a word, including the example sentence and usage notes, to ensure I'm not accidentally deleting something essential. The words I take are wispy things, with only one or two definitions. A couple targeted swipes of the eraser and *poof*! Gone.

For one fleeting moment, after I catch Jay scratching a legful of angry pink mosquito bites during English, I consider erasing all bugs, not just wasps. Jay is allergic to mosquitoes—

she used to puff up like a blowfish every summer when we'd spend hours in Sasha's backyard. The only thing that gave her any relief was calamine lotion, so she'd slather it over her bites and walk around from June to August covered in huge white spots.

"I'm like a human Bambi," she'd groan. Sash and I called her Jambi.

But then I realize—and this strikes me like a thunderbolt to the chest—that if I erased *all* bugs, it might take Lightning Bugs, too.

Sorry, Jay. Bugs must stay.

⊙

There's only one hiccup in an otherwise perfect morning. En route to lunch, I overhear a couple of guys at their lockers talking about a pool party. My knees, normally bone-like, devolve quickly into paste.

All morning I've been hopped up on power, the secret word vigilante of Ryden Junior High. I am indomitable. And invomitable, meaning I haven't once felt queasy. For the first time in ages, I forget all about the Shadoom for three consecutive hours.

But there it is. Circling me in the dark water, fin just visible above the surface.

I frown. Didn't I already erase POOL? A memory knocks

around my skull: me hunched over in the locker room, cold fingers running the babáki over the page.

I have to know. With a furtive glance over my shoulder, I dart into the empty science lab.

When I flip to POMERANIAN ⊙ POOR MAN'S CABBAGE, it's halfway down the page, smirking up at me.

pool |ˈpül|
noun

> 1 a puddle of standing liquid
> 2 a swimming pool

My pulse pounds in my ear canals. It's alarming how much this alarms me. What's the big deal? I must have only erased one *kind* of pool. This is easy to fix.

But I can't shake the feeling that the dictionary is toying with me. That just when I think I'm safe, I won't be safe at all.

My hands are trembling as I erase *all* the words this time. The pronunciation. The part of speech. The first definition, then the second. I take all of it, leaving no room for error.

When I'm done, the Shadoom is quiet. My breath begins to smooth. The shark has stopped stalking its prey.

Sure it has, says the persnickety voice in my head. *For now.*

I remove my glasses. Huff warm air onto the lenses and rub

them on my shirt. But I must be doing it wrong, because the yellow suns on the rim don't get any brighter.

The persnickety voice is right. My triumph, so shiny only a few minutes ago, is tarnished. I've won a temporary victory, not a lasting defeat.

Slowly, cautiously, I begin to page through the dictionary. There must be other potential triggers. Other words I can erase.

I consider NIGHT, but decide against it. Same with DARK. People need to sleep. Animals need to prowl. Even if I don't personally thrive at nighttime, there are plenty of reasons the sun should not shine 24-7. All things being equal, I'd prefer *not* to upset the cosmos, a word that derives from the Greek word *kosmos*, meaning "the whole orderly universe."

Then there's SHADOW.

If you slice the Shadoom in half, you wind up with two parts: *shadows* + *room*. I don't think I can get away with erasing all rooms, not unless I want to transform Ryden Junior High into a vast, cavernous space with no walls and no privacy.

But shadows? Are there any good reasons for keeping those?

The dictionary cedes an entire page to SHADE and SHADOW. Twenty-three definitions of SHADOW (noun) and thirteen of SHADOW (verb), plus dozens of hybrids, not all of them familiar: SHADOW NUCLEUS, SHADOW PAINTING, SHADOW SKIRT. The whole word family gives me the shivers—phantoms and dark figures and the shadow of death.

And then something strange happens.

No matter how many times I drag the babáki over the shadow words, I can't erase them.

I rub harder, increasingly unsettled. But nothing changes. As if these particular words have been inscribed in indelible ink.

The C. *Scuro Dictionary* won't let me take any of them. Not even after I give it a punishing finger flick.

"We seem to be at an impasse," I growl.

Then I page emphatically to I—and erase IMPASSE.

Zia: I. Dictionary: I.

It still won't surrender SHADOW. But at least it knows I'm capable of fighting back.

potado |pə-ˈtā-dō|
noun

   ɪ a whirling vortex of violently rotating tubers

   From English *potato*, "edible starchy tuber," and *tornado*, "a whirling vortex of violently rotating winds."

"Zia!"

Alice struts toward me down the hall. The moment I see her tangerine bomber jacket and Alicious swagger—a swagger that's deliciously Alice—a smile starts tugging at my cheeks.

Look at that. I just made up a new word.

Still got it.

"So," Alice says, matching my stride as I walk to the cafeteria. She falls in step beside me so naturally it's like we do this all the time. "On a scale of one to forty-seven, how would you rate your morning?"

"Forty-eight." I consider my petulant dictionary and revise. "On second thought: forty-six point five."

"I see." She nods gravely. "A tragic one-point-five loss in the final inning. The coach decides to punt."

"Did you just mix up a bunch of different sports?"

She grins, sheepish.

"Friend confession time: I don't know the first thing about sports."

I can't help it. When she says *friend*, a swarm of butterflies lands in my spleen.

"What do you think?" Alice says as we approach the cafeteria. "Should we brave the wild today? Sit at a table?"

"A *table*?" I gasp in mock horror. "Like normal humans who sit in chairs?"

"We don't have to be *normal*. We just have to sit in chairs."

I let out a long, languorous sigh. "If we must."

Alice takes the lead, and I follow, hoping she can't hear my heart thudding in my throat.

Maybe my horror wasn't so mock.

There's a unique terror that comes from three hundred junior high kids crammed into one big echoey cafeteria. For starters, it's loud. Talk-laugh-shout-giggle-squeal-brag-chew-slurp-flirt-fart loud. Not to mention the school hierarchy is on full display. I call it the Junior High-archy. In fifth grade all the tables were on the same level, but now there's an elevated platform in the center of the cafeteria, with one long table where all the popular kids sit. That way weirdlings like me can gaze up at the royals while eating our lowly string cheese.

These days it's worse. There are landmines everywhere. Sasha and Jay at our old table, staring me down. Thom Strong and his disciples, either bullies themselves or guys who figure being "friends" with a bully offers some sort of blanket protection.

"I see Luis." Alice waves at Luis Lopez, who's sitting alone at a ground-floor table. I didn't know Alice knew him. She seems to know everyone, even though she's new.

We head to the table to drop off our stuff.

"Hey, guys!" Luis says, clearly relieved to no longer be alone. I guess he doesn't sit with Sasha and Jay anymore, either. "Science was cool today, right, Zia? I can't wait till we move out of arthropods and into amphibians. Mr. Brockmeier says my mom can come as a special guest."

Luis talks a lot about reptiles and amphibians. His mom is a famous herpetologist, so Dr. Lopez talks a lot about reptiles and amphibians, too, only she does it on TV. Luis says his mom once held a frog in one hand and a salamander in the other while signing autographs. It's called being amphibextrous.

The other thing he talks about is musicals. You wouldn't think those things go together, but for Luis Lopez, they do.

"Hey, Luis," Alice says. "Are you nervous about auditions today?"

He cocks his head. "About what?"

"Don't you have auditions for the musical?"

I cock my head, too. For a split second I thought I understood what she was asking. But then that second split.

Alice blinks at me, then Luis. "Why are you both staring at me like that?"

"Mrs. Harrison posts the cast list for the musical today," Luis says slowly. "If that's what you mean."

Alice throws up her hands. "Sure." She turns to me. "Want to get food, Z?"

I nod, and she steers me toward the lunch line.

"*That* was awkward," she mutters. I grunt noncommittally, not wanting to admit Alice used a word I didn't know.

Luckily, she shifts gears. "Guess what day it is, Z?"

"Wednesday?"

"That, too. But today's our *lucky* Wednesday, because: chicken fingers!"

I skid to a stop.

Most days Mom packs my lunch. She says there's no reason to eat cafeteria food when a brown-bag lunch is adequate and nutritious. The truth, of course, is that cafeteria food is expensive.

But on the rare occasions I do eat cafeteria food, I'm on what they call Reduced Lunch. Mom will tuck a couple bucks into my backpack with a note scrawled on a bev nap: "Go hog wild, Sunshine Girl!" She always draws a heart.

Hog wild is, as it turns out, ironic. When you're on Reduced Lunch you can only buy certain foods, and bacon, carnitas, and pulled pork are definitely not among them. All the good stuff is off limits: chicken fingers, pizza, tacos, spaghetti, nachos with plastastic orange cheese. Instead you get to choose from a fine assortment of gloopy mashed potatoes, vegetable medley, and a wiggly white fish called scrod that makes me lose hope for humanity.

"Actually," I say, "*you* get chicken fingers. I'm in more of a scrod mood myself."

Alice arches an eyebrow as I walk swiftly to the Reduced Lunch line, feeling appropriately reduced.

I'm spooning a gray glob of potatoes onto my fish when someone bumps into my shoulder. I look up. My hands go cold.

"Nice scrod," says Thom Strong. "Ever play bumper trays?"

He bangs my tray with his tray—and my plate goes flying.

If you've never lost an entire plate of scrod and mashed potatoes to a cafeteria floor, I would not recommend it. They don't just splat on the ground. There's a vortex effect as they spray outward, spattering all shoes and legs within a five-foot radius.

Everyone around me shrieks and jumps back. I hear an impressive array of swear words. Kids stare. Glare. I'm glued in place, unable to make my legs move.

Maybe I *should* have erased potatoes. Or trays.

Out of the corner of my eye, I catch a glimpse of Thom. To my surprise, he isn't gloating. His face is frozen in a funny expression. Like maybe he didn't expect bumper trays to end this way.

"Back off, Thom." Alice is standing by my side. "You can't treat people like that."

Thom's face closes up again. "Shove it, Phan. Go stick some patches on your ugly jacket."

He storms off with his tray of scrod.

Only then does it dawn on me that Thom is on Reduced Lunch, too.

"It's all right, girls." One of the cafeteria ladies is scuttling toward us with a mop. "I'll take care of this. You go enjoy your lunch."

Considering my lunch is dappling the ankles of at least ten people, *enjoy* doesn't seem like the opportune word.

Alice holds out her hand. "Come with me, Zia."

And finally, my legs begin to move.

⊙

"I can't believe he did that." Alice paces the girls' restroom in short, jagged steps. "What an unconscionable jerk."

I nod my head in fierce agreement, even though *unconscionable* is yet another word Alice knows that I don't.

"I'm scared of him," I admit.

"Of Thom? That guy's a joke!"

"Yeah, but he's a *mean* joke."

Alice stops pacing. "You want to know something? I bet *he's* scared. My dad says that when kids treat each other badly, it's almost always because of fear. They're afraid of people who seem different. I think Thom hasn't figured out that being a weirdling is actually cool."

She grabs a fistful of brown paper towels from the dispenser. "Here. Let's get you cleaned up."

She runs the towels under the faucet before handing them over. I bend down to wipe off my shins, offering a silent apology to the potatoes. No potato deserves this.

"I'm not like you, Alice," I say quietly. "You stand up to bullies and wear cool bomber jackets, and you're not scared of anything."

Alice lets out a short, sharp laugh.

"I wish that were true," she says.

"Isn't it?"

She leans hard into the towel dispenser.

"I'll tell you something I'm scared of. My mom is about to have a baby. I've been an only child my whole life, and—fine—maybe I'm a little bit spoiled. But for months all she and my dad have talked about is baby, baby, baby. I'm scared of . . ." She exhales. "I'm scared they're going to forget about me."

Alice blows hair out of her eyes.

"You want to know the real reason I told Sasha I couldn't come over to her house? It's because I had other plans that night. I joined the Ryden Story Club. I've been working on a stand-up routine."

My eyebrows skyrocket above my glasses. "Really?"

"I want to be a comedian. I figure if I can make people laugh . . . if I can make my *parents* laugh . . . then maybe I won't be invisible."

She gives me a shy smile. I didn't know *shy* was in Alice Phan's vocabulary. I also didn't know we had so much in common. She likes making people laugh, too.

"You don't seem invisible to me." I swab the last speck of scrod off my shoe. "You're not scared of being onstage in front of all those people?"

She stands an inch taller. "You told me what you want, so now it's my turn: I don't want to be afraid."

82

"Is it that easy? You just say it and then, *boom*, you're not afraid?"

"Maybe." She tugs at the gray hair band around her wrist. Her shoulders shrink back down to normal Alice size. "I wish."

ombres chinoises |ˈämbrə ˌshēnˈwäz|
plural noun

1 shadows of puppets or persons thrown upon
a transparent screen and made to act a play: *In this
evening's ombres chinoises, the play's the thing wherein
I'll catch the conscience of my darkest dreams.*

The pink slip arrives in seventh period. Usually office aides deliver pink slips, but Mrs. Nelson brings this one herself.

"Your mom is running late today, honey." She hands me the slip. "You okay walking home?"

"It's fine," I say. "We only live a few blocks from here."

In the sense that *a few* means "ten," this is true. But I don't like the way Mrs. Nelson is looking at me. I don't want to be the charity case of Ryden Junior High.

So I walk home, which gives me plenty of time to replay my cafeteria shaming. Thom's mean face. Alice's brave face. The cafeteria lady's pity face. Worst of all, my own face in the bathroom mirror. Embarrassed. Scared.

How could such a promising morning turn into such a terrible afternoon?

I let myself into the apartment with my key—and find a note waiting. It's on the kitchen counter, pinned under the big blue bowl where fruit goes to die.

> Hi, Sunshine Girl!
> At the doctor with Yiayia. Should be back in an hour,
> two hours tops. Call me if you need a Lightning Bug!
> Love you to the stars and back. ☺
>
> Mom

I feel a telltale pinch, a door creaking on its hinges. Two hours is plenty of time for the sun to set and the Shadoom to creep into my chest.

No. That's not going to happen. I won't let it.

I take off my glasses and reach for a kitchen towel. My hand hovers over the one with orange kittens. *Marmalade cats,* Mom always says. *Aren't they cute?*

I choose the striped towel instead.

It helps, buffing the rims of my glasses. It's good to have something to do with my hands. When I'm done, the suns are bright and cheery yellow.

At least Mom left me a snack: Easy Peasy Mac-n-Cheesy, my favorite thing on The Sweet Potato's menu. I feel a sudden swell of gratitude that I did not erase RESTAURANT after all.

I peel off the *15 min. at 375°* Post-it note, open the oven door, and set the dish of Mac-n-Cheesy on a wire rack. Our oven is gas, not electric, so when I crank the knob I hear the soft pop of flames. Mom says a gas stovetop is dangerous, but obviously I don't touch the burners. I'm not in kindergarten.

Mouseimus slinks between my ankles. When I scoop him off the linoleum, he curves into my arms like a big furry cashew.

"Mr. Mouse is in the house." I kiss his cold wet nose. "Not a shabby tabby."

Even if the sun is hurtling toward the horizon, I'm not alone. I've got Gluteus Mouseimus to keep me company.

Soon I'll have some Mac-n-Cheesy. Everything is going to be just fine.

Tap. My stomach twists. *Tap. Tap.*

"I must be hungry!" I say aloud, like maybe I can convince myself it's true. All day long the Shadoom has kept its distance. Why should now be any different?

I sink into Yiayia's purple rocking chair and fold Mr. Mousie into my lap. I feel his heart beating. Or maybe that's mine.

Two hours. Two hours is nothing, right? Easy Peasy Light-n-Breezy.

I don't even last two minutes.

At first it's cold. Mouseimus's fur is always toasty, but as he sits on my lap, a chill shivers up my arms. I hug him closer, trying to absorb his warmth. When I press my face into his fluffy belly, he mews and pats my cheek with his paw.

It's the sweetest, kindest, absolute worst thing Mr. Mousie could do.

The images come one after another, as vivid as they were on the screen in Sasha's backyard. The mama tuxedo cat with her black fur and white boots. Her little gray kitten prancing along behind her. The car that comes out of nowhere.

The mama reaching out one crushed paw, touching her baby's face to say goodbye.

The memories rush in as our apartment fades away. I'm standing on a patio with balloons tied to the chairs. I'm wading into dark blue water. I'm staring up at the movie screen, sharp blades of grass sticking to the backs of my thighs.

The night of Sasha's party.

⊙

"She's here!" Sasha cries. "Z's here!"

The second I step onto the patio, Sash and Jay move toward me in slow motion. We do this whenever we see each other. An exaggerated run at half speed, accompanied by an equally drawn-out "ZASHAYYYYYYY!" It always ends with a melodramatic embrace, the three of us fake sobbing. *I thought I'd never see you again. I've just missed you so much. Please never leave me.* We call it our Greet-Cute.

"ZASHAYYYYYYY!" Sasha and Jay slow-shout at me.

"ZASHAYYYYYYY!" I slow-shout back, pumping my arms as I inch-run alongside the pool. We slow-collide so awkwardly I nearly fall over.

"Careful!" I say, laughing. "You almost knocked me into the pool."

"It's a pool party," Sasha says, deadpan.

"Yeah but at least let me take my shorts off first!"

"Those shorts are *so* cute," Jay raves, and Sasha rolls her eyes.

"C'mon, Mom's setting up the screen. It's a kids' movie—not the one *I* wanted, let the record show. But it's the only movie my parents would let us watch with the littles here."

The littles are Sasha's younger sisters, Heaven and Nevaeh. No matter how much she pretends they annoy her, it's clear she adores them.

"Where are the burritos?" Jay says. "You promised us burritos."

"Ugh, be patient! Dad's setting up the burrito bar. Just save room for dessert." She winks. "He's got peach cobbler in the oven."

Jay and I exchange wordless glances, confirming that yes, we will both be sneaking into the kitchen to steal an extra spoonful of peach cobbler before the night is out.

The funny thing is, I do sneak into the kitchen. Just not the way I thought. My night ends much earlier than anyone expected.

In another way, though, the night never ends. I'm still inside it.

I don't know when it started, exactly. It's hard for me to pinpoint the exact moment. It must have been during the movie, after the scene where the mama cat dies. I remember the giant screen going black at the edges. At first I thought the projector had broken, but when I looked around, no one else batted an eye. It was just me. I watched, helpless, as an ominous dark rectangle closed in around the screen, choking out the light frame by frame.

It felt slow at first, and then it wasn't slow at all. When

Sasha and Jay and the rest of the girls jumped into the pool, whooping and splashing, I felt like I was sinking. Like I was being dragged to the deep end by some dark invisible force I couldn't name.

It was the Shadoom, of course. I know that now. But all I knew that night was that something inside me was casting a long shadow. Food turned dark in my mouth. Laughter turned dark in my ears. The smell of peaches turned dark in my nose.

I could feel myself shrinking away from everyone and everything. I was going through the motions, but my bones had gone numb. After a while I was so exhausted from pretending to be normal, I found a chair on the patio and sat in it alone.

Mrs. Davis came out to check on me.

"You okay, Zia? You get enough to eat?"

"Mm," I said. I must not have been very convincing, because she disappeared and reemerged a minute later with a big slab of cobbler on a paper plate.

As I stared at the oozing peaches, my eyes filled with tears.

I had to get out of there before I completely fell apart. The last thing Sasha needed on her birthday was me having a total meltdown. While everyone crowded around the patio table to light Sasha's purple candles and sing "Happy Birthday," I slipped inside the house. I tiptoed into Mr. and Mrs. Davis's bedroom, where I used the cordless phone to call Mom's cell.

Hi! You've reached Sophia. Hi! You've reached Sophia. Hi! You've reached—

I must've called twenty times before I realized it was useless. Mom always kept her phone in the back during her shifts at The Sweet Potato.

By the time I tiptoed back into the kitchen, Sasha's dad was at the sink, washing dishes and humming to the smooth jazz pouring from a speaker.

"Mr. Davis?"

"Hey there, Zia!" He turned off the faucet. "I didn't know you were inside."

I swallowed hard. I wasn't sure how many words I could manage without crying.

"Can you take me to The Sweet Potato?"

And he did. He left his own daughter's birthday party to drive me. I told him I needed to go *now*, and he didn't ask any questions. I'll always love Mr. Davis for that.

The minute I saw Mom in her orange apron, holding an order of fries, I burst into tears.

"Sunshine Girl!" she cried, dropping the whole plate of fries. "Are you okay?"

I didn't answer. I was most definitely not okay.

Mom scooped me up in a mama-bear hug and took me to the kitchen, where she told her manager she was going on break. We went out the back door and into the parking lot, where we climbed into the Brownie. I hadn't sat on Mom's lap in a long time, but that night, tucked into the back seat of our station wagon, I did. She held me, stroking my back, while I sobbed.

Mom kept asking if the other girls had been mean to me. "Did they say something, Zia? Did they hurt you?"

All I could do was shake my head. *No. No.* A part of me wished Sasha and Jay *had* been mean. At least then I could explain why I felt this way.

Over and over, Mom asked, "What's wrong, sweet girl? What is it?"

Over and over, I answered, "I don't know."

I didn't know that night, or the night after. Or the night after that.

Later, when I apologized for the dropped fries, Mom said, "It's okay. It was only a matter of time. That's just the way I am."

I think about that a lot. I know Mom was trying to make me feel better, but her words haunt me. There's so much truth in them. Some things lurk deep inside us, and they'll come out eventually, no matter how hard we fight.

It was only a matter of time.

That's just the way I am.

☉

The memory cracks me wide open.

I'm frozen in Yiayia's rocking chair, shadows swirling in and around me, tearing through my body like a tornado. The darkness seeps into the hollows of my rib cage. It oozes through my blood.

The Shadoom is outside me, inside me. It's everywhere.

I should call Mom. Ask for a Lightning Bug. Beg her to come home. The Shadoom blots out everything good and sweet and easy. It hurts too much to bear the weight of that alone.

The cordless phone is only six steps away. Three if I leap them.

But what would I tell Mom? Even if I *did* find the words, then she'd know her Sunshine Girl was broken. And what if even she can't fix me?

That would be so much worse.

I hear a soft flutter. The sound of paper ruffling in my backpack.

The dictionary.

My hands ache to hold it. I know it's calling for me, offering to conjure its magic. But my bag is crumpled on the floor by the kitchen counter, which feels like miles from where I am. My chest is shrinking, folding in on itself like a paper napkin. Soon there will be nothing left.

The fifteen-minute mark worms past, then another fifteen. The Mac-n-Cheesy is burning in the oven. I can smell it.

The oven is so close, but I can't reach it, can't even stand up, because the Shadoom has replaced every molecule of my blood with cement. Before long, smoke will pour out the sides. The kitchen will catch on fire, and I will sizzle to crisps, right here in this chair, and Gluteus Mouseimus will sizzle to crisps, too, all because I was powerless to save him.

Why does this happen? I hear the other sixth-grade girls talk about who likes whom and when they'll be allowed to shave their legs. Sure, they have bad days. But most of the time, they're sunny. And here I am, too scared to leave my grandmother's rocking chair.

Other people seem to have feelings, while my feelings have me.

The pricklies rise on my arm like bumps on a strawberry. I'm afraid of losing Mom. Afraid of being alone, but also afraid of being with people. Afraid they won't understand the Shadoom, that they'll think I'm weird or messed up, that something is seriously wrong with me. I guess, at the heart of it, I'm afraid they're right.

How have I never seen it? I know the name of the Shadoom. The *real* name, not the one I made up.

Fear.

It's always been fear, but the shadows made it too dark to see.

Mouseimus slides off my lap with a disgruntled meow as I force myself up. I turn off the oven, quietly apologizing to the

Mac-n-Cheesy on the rack inside, which is now the Mac-n-Charredy.

Then I tug the *C. Scuro Dictionary* out of my backpack and dig a finger into F.

This time, the dictionary doesn't stop me. It opens right to the page I want.

fear |ˈfir|
noun

    ɪ an emotion caused by impending danger, evil, etc., whether the threat is real or imagined; the feeling or condition of being afraid: *What would it be like to live without fear?*

My cheeks flush hot. There it is. While I've been wasting time erasing silly, unimportant things, the word I wanted was right here all along.

There's movement on the page.

The ink beads beneath my fingertips. An illustration materializes on the paper, bubbly like a comic book. A dark-haired girl sits alone on a canopy bed, three hair bands gracing her left wrist.

Alice.

She stands, her cartoon eyes catching mine. Suddenly she's moving toward me at an alarming speed, her picture growing larger, as if she desperately needs to tell me something. I hold my breath. Is she going to step right off the page?

But then the ink contorts, twisting into a starburst, and Alice vanishes inside the whorl.

Her words echo in my head.

I don't want to be afraid.

It's so obvious it might as well be inked onto my eyelids. Yiayia is afraid of cars and mountain lions. Mom is afraid of losing her job. Alice is afraid her parents are going to forget about her. Even Thom Strong is afraid—afraid of people who are different.

And me?

That's easy. I'm afraid of everything.

But I don't have to be. Not anymore.

I'm breathing hard as I lift the eraser from the dictionary. This time I don't hesitate.

I press the babáki into FEAR.

I erase every letter.

naucify |ˈnôs-ə-fī|

verb *[obsolete]*

I

"Wake up, Sunshine Girl."

Mom is sitting on the edge of my bed. Warm, buttery sunlight pours through the window.

I rub my eyes, head still foggy.

"You conked out early last night, Z! You were fast asleep in Yiayia's rocking chair when we got home. I had to carry you to bed."

My chest feels funny. Like someone took one of those fireplace puffers and puffed extra air between my ribs. It's a strange sensation . . . and kind of nice.

"I made pancakes," Mom says. "And eggs. Slow scrambled with butter and cheese, just the way you like."

We never have a sit-down breakfast in the morning. "Won't we be late?"

She shrugs. "I have four words for you: banana and chocolate chip."

Mom stands, stretches, and catches her reflection in the full-length mirror on the closet door. She's wearing her hair down for the first time in months, and it swishes over her shoulders in long black waves. She lifts herself on her tiptoes, going up, up, up, until she's taller than I've ever seen her. Her face is different, too. Brighter.

She smiles as she drops back down onto her heels.

"I haven't done that in ages."

"What's it called?"

"Ballet."

She sashays down the hall, calling over her shoulder, "Hotcakes won't stay hot forever . . ."

Instantly, all the head fog evaporates. I jerk upright and grab my glasses off the nightstand, remembering the trail of blue rubber worms the eraser left as I raked it across FEAR.

Mom isn't afraid of being late to work at the dance studio, because she isn't afraid of anything.

It *worked*.

I leap out of bed, stripping off yesterday's clothes. When I smell my armpits, they're not terrible, so I skip the shower, throw on jeans, and make my way to the kitchen.

Where I grind to a halt.

There's a new kitchen table, sheeny and varnished oak, with big knobby legs and four chairs. And there's food on the table—*real* food. Cheesy eggs, chocolate-chip-banana pancakes, and a pitcher of fresh-squeezed orange juice. As in, Mom squeezed real-life oranges with her real-life hands.

Yiayia sits at the head of the table, beaming. She has a napkin tucked into her blouse, and her lipstick looks fresh.

"Do you like the table?" Mom hands me a glass of OJ. "I got it for a steal. Only two hundred dollars!"

I spit-take the OJ. Two hundred bucks may be cheap for a table, but it's not cheap for Mom.

And yet somehow, I'm not worried.

"Zioula mou!" Yiayia beckons me closer. "Éla, come sit with your yiayia. We have the hot cake!"

I slide into my varnished chair, pondering that age-old question: Why do people call pancakes hotcakes? It's not like you fry them in a hot. A quandary of this magnitude requires sustenance, so I fork a pancake onto my plate, watching the yellow slab of butter melt perfectly over its beautiful chocolate-studded surface.

Mom is squeezing more orange juice. The electric juicer hums from the kitchen.

"Yiayia," I say. "Are you afraid of mountain lions?"

She peers at me intently. Something sparks in her brown eyes. I lean forward instinctively, ready for her to drop some powerful Greek wisdom.

Instead, she laughs. "What you mean, paidaki mou? I have always the mountains."

I feel a burst of triumph.

"How about cars? Are you scared of cars?"

My grandmother smiles serenely. "What is this, *scared*?"

Mr. Mousie jumps onto the new table, and no one shoos him off. He plops down by the cheesy eggs and starts licking his furry paws. His tummy is temptingly white and fluffy, so I rub it.

The fear of losing Mouseimus and Mom, of being alone forever—all gone.

I want to shout with joy. Eat six thousand pancakes. Scoop the sun out of the sky and use it as a nightlight.

But I don't need a nightlight. I'm no longer afraid of the night.

⊙

Things get even better at school.

Thanks to the pancakes-and-OJ bonanza, I'm late to science. But Mr. Brockmeier doesn't care. He's wearing llama pajamas.

"Miss Zia Angelis! Zia of the Angels! Your celestial seat awaits."

I slip into my celestial seat, stowing my bulbous, dictionary-sized backpack under my feet. Luis flashes me a thumbs-up from across the room. I flash one back.

"Today we're changing things up," says Mr. B. "Filing past a few phyla, if you know what I mean. It's a new kind of evolution, straight from Arthropoda to Chordata. Hey, that almost rhymes!" He rubs his hands together. "Who wants to watch a movie?"

Everyone wants to watch a movie.

"Glad to know I've got a class of film buffs," Mr. B says. He points to his pj's. "As you may have guessed, today is all about llamas."

Mr. Brockmeier *loves* llamas. He owns at least six different llama ties and gets a little teary when he talks about the year he spent with a wool shaman in a yurt in Peru. Llamas are in the camel family, and Mr. B's first name is Samuel.

By now it should be obvious why we call him Samel the Camel behind his back.

That one was all me. But I wasn't making fun. I actually think he'd be delighted.

"Today we'll be watching *The Llegacy of the Llama*," says Samel the Camel as he plugs his phone into the projector and the title pops onto the screen. "It's one of my all-time favorites."

It occurs to me Samel the Camel might play llama documentaries every day if it weren't for fear. Which begs the question: What is he afraid of? Getting called into the principal's office? Phone calls from angry parents?

And another thing. How do I still remember fear? I can't remember the other words I erased. Unlike FEAR, they didn't stick around for long. Then again, they weren't very big words. In honor of Mr. Brockmeier, here's a scientific hypothesis: maybe the truly big ideas take longer to erode.

Because the truth is, even though I can still hold *fear* in my mind, it's beginning to feel like an obscure word. Obscure words are ones that still exist in the dictionary, but most people have forgotten them. *Lickspittle. Toadeater. Cumberworld.*

I read somewhere that it's only a matter of time before an

obscure word becomes obsolete. Once that happens, the word is removed from the dictionary. It used to make me sad. The idea of little *toadeater*, lonely and forgotten, vanishing into the Great Toad Beyond.

But now that I've removed a few words myself, I feel differently. Words exist to help us understand and describe the world around us. If no one remembers what they mean, then they're not really helping anyone.

The way I see it, sometimes that's the absolute best thing a word can do.

Vanish into the Great Word Beyond.

⊙

We do not leave the llamas behind in science class. They trot right along to art, where Ms. Mundinger has us draw them in pastels.

"They're such gorgeous creatures," she says, eyes sparkling. "So masculine and strong!"

I happen to think they look like feather dusters with eyes and teeth, but that's the thing about art: it's subjective.

I'm counting down the minutes until lunch. I can't wait to find Alice and ask how her day has been. *On a scale of one to forty-seven* . . .

When the bell rings, I bolt out of my seat and race down the hall, flying past the girls' restroom. What's so scary about the cafeteria? My chest feels light as air, stuffed with cotton candy and sunbeams.

Luis is alone again, so I make a beeline for his table.

"Did you see Snape in science today?" he says, skipping right over "hello."

"Who?"

"Snape! My ball python. I mean, I have two ball pythons, obviously. But Snape is more extroverted."

Now I remember: Luis has a ball python named Snape the Snake. Props on a killer pet name.

"I brought him to school," he says.

"I thought you weren't allowed?"

Earlier this year, Luis told our class about the time he brought Snape the Snake for show-and-tell in second grade and a girl got so freaked out she had an asthma attack. Since then, Snape has stayed at home eating pinkie mice and sunning himself on a rock.

"Today my mom said it was okay. Snape's chillin' in Mr. B's room under a heat lamp." Luis laughs at his own joke. "Get it? Chillin'? *Heat* lamp?"

"Hey, guys." And there she is. Alice Phan, wearing a peacock-purple bomber jacket. "This seat taken?"

My smile could fill every page of the C. *Scuro Dictionary.*

"It's all yours."

Alice drops her backpack next to mine. But before I can say anything, someone yells from across the cafeteria.

"Phan! Hey, Phan!"

Thom Strong is charging toward us.

"PHAN! I've got something to say to you."

Normally I clench up the moment I see him. Not today.

Thom looms over our table, red-faced. Alice stands so their eyes meet. I stand, too.

"Okay then." She folds her arms over her chest. Fearless. "Say it."

He wipes his mouth on his sleeve.

"I . . . I'm sorry."

mominous | ˈmä-mə-ˈnəs|
adjective

1 when moms start acting strangely, giving the impression that something bad is about to happen: *I can't quite shake the mominous feeling in my gut.*

From English *mom,* "abbreviation of *momma,*" and Latin *ominosus,* "a bad omen."

That's right. Thomas J. Strong—school villain and asinine bully—just apologized.

Alice cocks her head. "You're sorry?"

"Uh. Yeah."

"Sorry for what?"

Thom kicks the table leg with his sneaker. "For saying what I said about your jacket. That wasn't cool."

Alice looks at me, then back at Thom.

"What about Zia?" she says. "You owe her an apology."

Thom rubs the back of his buzz cut, clearly uncomfortable. "I wasn't trying to turn your lunch into a potato bomb, Angelis. And I'm sorry I say mean stuff."

I never thought I'd hear the word *sorry* from Thom Strong. A fresh wave of confidence washes over me. I poke my glasses farther up my nose and stand taller, shimmery and strong.

"Thank you," I say.

I notice a purple smudge on the inside of his wrist. When he catches me staring, he yanks his shirtsleeve down to cover it.

"We cool, guys?" he says.

Alice unfolds her arms. "Are you going to stop being asinine?"

"Sure." Thom grins. "As soon as I figure out what that means."

He salutes Alice, then me, then pulls his phone out of his

pocket and blasts heavy metal as he head-bangs his way out of the cafeteria.

I will never understand boys.

"You guys," Luis says as Alice and I sit. "Check out Samel the Camel and Ms. M."

The secret love affair between Mr. Brockmeier and Ms. Mundinger is the stuff of school legend, though up till now it's been mere speculation. They're younger than most of our teachers, they wear neon sneakers, and they're both really into llamas. Rumor has it they were once seen flirting in the faculty parking lot. Everyone calls them Mr. and Mrs. Brockmundian, though I prefer my ship name: the Cameldinger.

Today, myth has become reality in the school cafeteria. There, by the salad bar, Ms. Mundinger sweeps Samel the Camel into her arms with so much passion the plastic bin of croutons flies into the ranch.

"Revolting," Alice says, right as I say, "Repulsive."

She cackles with glee. "We keep doing that."

"I know, right? It's like we have the same—"

"Thesaurus," she finishes. "By the way, there's a snake in the cafeteria."

"What?"

I look where she's pointing to see that there is, in fact, an enormous ball python slithering across the floor.

"Poop," says Luis.

When Luis told us his snake was five feet long, he wasn't kidding. If you stood Snape on one end, he'd be as tall as my mom. I actually think snakes are cool, but I understand why people are scared of them. It's something about the way they move. That coiling liquid s.

At the moment there is a massive five-foot python liquid-s-ing through the cafeteria, wriggling around backpacks and purses and chair legs, sliding over the feet of hundreds of junior high schoolers . . . and not a single one of them is freaking out.

They should be shrieking, jumping on tables, knocking over milk cartons. Instead, kids point and giggle and move their backpacks out of the way so Snape has a clear path. Someone starts clapping, and soon the whole cafeteria erupts into cheers. Luis goes after him, but once he realizes he's got everyone's attention, he starts hamming it up, narrating Snape's actions like a sports commentator. Which just makes everybody laugh harder.

No wonder Luis does school musicals. He's a natural. Even Mr. Brockmeier and Ms. Mundinger stop canoodling long enough to applaud.

"Look!" I say. "Even the Cameldinger loves it!"

Alice snorts with laughter. "The Cameldinger! That's too good. Could I use it for my set?"

"Sure!" I flourish a bow. "I have no idea what that is."

"Oh, sorry, obnoxious comedy talk. A five-minute 'set'

is basically just a stand-up routine. Story Club is hosting a jamboree after school tomorrow, so I've been writing new jokes."

She slaps the table, suddenly inspired.

"You should sign up, Zia! You can do anything you want—it doesn't have to be comedy. It's basically an open mic where you get onstage and tell a story to the audience."

I think of the Lightning Bug stories Mom tells me at night, how they help fight off the Shadoom. Right now the Shadoom feels like a faraway story, some spooky tale Jay or Sasha told at a slumber party with flashlights under the blanket fort when we were kids.

"You seem like you'd be good at telling stories," Alice says. "You're a natural wordsmith. And you're funny. I don't think you know how funny you are."

Usually when I think about speaking onstage in front of a big group of people, all the moisture in my mouth evaporates. Sorry, folks! The saliva has left the building.

I wait for my mouth to turn into a giant cotton ball.

It doesn't.

"I don't even know what story I'd tell."

"Then come over today after school. You can tell a few practice stories, see which one feels right. My parents won't mind. My mom's at the hospital, but my dad's picking me up."

My eyes widen. "Your mom went into labor?"

"No, no. My mom's an ob-gyn, an obstetrician gynecologist. So basically a baby doc. She's been on maternity leave for the last few weeks, but for some reason today she woke up and decided to see patients. A baby doc who's having a baby. Talk about meta."

Alice really is intimidatingly good at this whole word thing. I make a mental note to look up *meta* in the dictionary later.

"My dad said we could make chè trôi nước tonight," she says. "It's a Vietnamese dessert with sticky rice balls in syrup. You could help us! It's *so* good." She pauses. "It'll be fun. I promise."

She sounds scared I might say no. But I must be hearing things. Alice can't be scared, because scared doesn't exist.

I feel a hopeful tickle in my chest. What if Alice is right? What if I'm good at telling stories? A story is made of words, and words are kind of my thing.

"I have to ask my mom."

"Sure. Here." She slides her phone across the table. It looks glossy and new. "Knock yourself out."

I call Mom, and it goes to voicemail. But the second time, she picks up.

"Fine with me," she says when I ask if I can go home with Alice. She sounds distracted. "That's great, actually—there's a drum circle I want to go to tonight."

"Drum circle?" I hear hip-hop music blaring in the

background. "Aren't you at The Sweet Potato?"

"I played hooky. I've been in the spare room at the studio all day."

"Doing what?"

"Dancing!" She laughs. "I couldn't believe it, Z. It was *fun*."

"I thought you said you couldn't do something for fun once you started doing it for money?"

"You sure do have a lot of questions."

It's true. I do. But with Mom's voice crackling audibly through Alice's phone speaker, now is not the time to ask them.

"Send me the Phans' address," Mom says. "I'll come get you after the drum circle. Have fun, Sunshine Girl!"

She hangs up before I can say anything. I'm left staring blankly at the phone.

"It's so weird," Alice says. "Why don't people ever drum in squares?"

That makes me laugh. Which is nice, because for the first time all day, I feel something dark slink through me. A wisp of a shadow.

Impossible. Without fear, there is no Shadoom.

I smack up against the same question I had during science. Why can I still remember fear? Not just the word, but the feeling. Even if I don't actively feel afraid, if I place my hand over my heart, I can conjure the shape of it. Almost like muscle memory.

New hypothesis. Maybe a Big-Deal word, with a For-

Serious idea behind it, doesn't switch off like a light. Maybe it's more like a light bulb in its final death throes. It dims, then brightens, dims, then brightens, before flickering out completely. And then, for a sliver of a moment, you see the shape of the light bulb burned onto your retinas before it all goes black.

Maybe fear is in its death throes.

Good. I can wait. I've waited my whole life not to be afraid. What's one more day?

$$\odot$$

"I'll show you a secret," I say to Alice.

We're in the locker room after seventh period, having just crushed another volleyball match. Our coach didn't show up today, so it was Alice, me, and a handful of other volleyball fiends. Thom Strong was absent, too.

"I love your secrets," Alice says, and a thrill twirls through me.

Today's been one for the record books. We've had three separate fire drills, probably because kids keep setting off fire alarms. Look, I get it. We've all daydreamed about pulling that little white handle, anointing ourselves with the metallic water from above. The handle literally says PULL DOWN.

Then Jay smiled at me in history, which hasn't happened in months, and there was an *actual* fire when someone mixed chemicals in the science lab to see if they'd explode. Along the way a bunch of teachers have walked out of their classrooms, including Mr. Brockmeier and Ms. Mundinger. Rumor has it the Cameldinger have eloped to start a llama farm in Peru.

Haven't seen Sasha recently, though. Come to think of it, I haven't seen Sasha all day.

"So what's the secret?" Alice says.

"I have to take you there."

"Okay." She swings her backpack over one shoulder. "Is it close by? It's just my dad is probably already in the carpool line . . ."

A text beeps on her phone. When she checks the screen, her mouth twists.

"Make that my *mom* in the carpool line. I guess my dad ended up being on call."

Glowering, she shoves her phone into the side pocket of her bag.

"This happens a lot. The worst is when they both get called in to the hospital, and they send someone to pick me up. Then I'm sort of just . . . on my own."

"Your dad's a doctor, too?" I realize there's a lot about Alice I don't know.

"Yeah. Different hospital. He's an emergency room doc." She smiles a little. "My dad calls himself Dr. Phan Number Two, because of course Mom is Dr. Phan Number One."

"Well then." I shoot her a conspiratorial look over the top

of my glasses. "I guess we'll have to share this secret with Dr. Phan Number One."

She peers at me, curious. I love that I've made Alice Phan curious. I lead her out of the locker room and down the back hallway, toward the door no one ever uses in the afternoons.

"My mom likes to avoid the Slow Drip of Parents. So we have a secret spot where we meet after school."

I'm giddily excited about showing Alice our secret spot. Even more excited about going home with her. I haven't been to a friend's house since Sasha's party.

Now when I think about that night, it's hard to remember what exactly went wrong.

"Text your mom to meet us in the far corner of the soccer field," I say over my shoulder. "By the blue bleachers."

I make a sharp turn into D Hall—and nearly trip over Sasha Davis.

She's huddled on the floor. Curled against the wall, hugging her knees to her chest, sobbing. In all the years we've been friends, I've seen Sasha cry maybe five times. I've never seen her sob. Not like this.

For a moment I forget all about Alice. It's just Sasha and me, the way it was up until first grade when we met Jay at gymnastics camp and Zasha became Zashay.

"Sash," I say softly, crouching beside her. "What's wrong?"

Her chest shudders. She peers up at me, then at Alice. A long moment passes.

"Oh. I . . ." Alice falters. "I think I'll just . . ."

Her phone rings, offering the perfect escape.

"Mom?" she says into the phone, hurrying down the hall to give us space.

I turn back to Sasha. Place a soothing hand on her arm.

"Hey. It's okay. Whatever it is, you can tell me."

I'm surprised at how easily I slip back into it, how natural it feels to be her friend.

But I don't think Sasha feels the same way. She chews her bottom lip, like she always does when she's deciding whether or not to trust someone.

"Mrs. Harrison just posted the cast list for the musical," she says, finally.

"Didn't you get the lead?"

She snorts. "I didn't even get a *part*. It's so unfair. It's always like this—Mrs. Harrison just assigns parts to her favorites, without giving the rest of us a chance. I'm a good singer, and I work hard. I wish there was some way I could show her what I can do."

My insides slide over an inch.

"You mean like a . . ."

I come up short. Why can't I remember the word I want?

Sasha needs a way to show Mrs. Harrison how good she is at singing. The fragment of a sentence flashes before my eyes. *A trial performance to win a role as . . .*

A. That's the first letter. I squeeze my eyes shut. *Au. Aud.*

Alice's voice bangs against my eardrums. She said the word yesterday at lunch, to Luis.

"An audible!" I shout.

No. That's not it.

"An auditorium?"

Closer, but still no.

Sasha blinks at me through the tears. "What are you even saying, Zia?"

I don't know what I'm saying, because I can't say it. The missing word is a *dot dot dot* snaking through my head.

Sasha holds my gaze. Like she's waiting for me to say something else. Something comforting. But I'm at a loss.

At the far end of the hall, I hear Alice open the door, then the suction-y sound as it closes behind her. I want to go after her. Ask her what word she said.

"Whatever." Sasha brushes the tears off her cheeks. "I don't want to be in the silly school musical anyway. I'll do my own thing."

She stands abruptly, swiping an arm across her face.

"I have to go. Jay will be waiting."

She leaves me alone in the empty hall.

luck | ˈlək|

noun

   1 a force that brings good fortune or adversity: *The matáki charm protects against mátiasma, the evil eye. Mátiasma brings bad luck.*

   2 the events or circumstances that operate for or against an individual: *If luck can be both good and bad, maybe being "lucky" isn't as great as it sounds.*

As we cut across the soccer fields, Alice keeps up a running monologue about how her mom just bought a new car, but only because her old car wasn't great for driving pregnant, and she wanted a bigger car anyway for when the baby comes, and, and, and . . .

I'm only half listening. I keep seeing Sasha's face, how betrayed she looked. I can't shake the feeling that what happened to her is somehow my fault.

". . . okay?" Alice asks.

It takes me a second to realize she's asked me a question.

"What? Sorry, I zoned out for a second."

"Is Sasha okay?"

I consider it. "I guess so? Honestly, I'm not sure."

Alice doesn't ask for details, which I appreciate. It's not just that I feel weird sharing Sasha's private heartache. It's that, when I try to recall the conversation, it goes blurry in my head. I feel like there was something I wanted to ask Alice, but as soon as we stepped outside, I couldn't remember what.

"There she is," she says, pointing to a sleek black SUV that definitely qualifies as a Rich Mom Car. An extra-pregnant woman waves from the driver's seat, the steering wheel resting comfortably on her belly.

"It's so nice to meet you, Zia," says Dr. Phan as Alice climbs into the front seat and I climb into the back. "Alice has told us a lot about you."

Alice rolls her eyes. "Not, like, a *lot*."

I can't help but grin. "It's nice to meet you, Dr. Phan Number One."

She smiles. "I see Alice has told you the family hierarchy."

Alice says something to her mom in Vietnamese. When Dr. Phan Number One responds, Alice speaks again, more sharply. This time her mom answers in one clipped word.

Alice and I lock eyes in the rearview mirror. Her mouth is tight around the edges.

"Mom says we can't make chè today. But maybe next time."

I feel a gooey cheese-melt of happy. *Next time.*

"Dr. Phan," I say, readying the question I've been mulling over since lunch. "Is it weird being a baby doctor when you're having your own baby? Is it like being a chef and eating your own cooking?"

She laughs. "Well, I don't plan to eat my own baby. But in the sense that I'm harder on myself, yes. I know exactly what I should and shouldn't be doing. I hold myself to a higher standard."

"Meaning it's all she thinks about," Alice mutters.

"Meaning I know all the things that could go wrong."

Alice snaps her hair bands. "Any more Braxton-Hicks contractions?"

"Not since yesterday." Dr. Phan sees my confusion in the rearview mirror. "Braxton-Hicks contractions aren't true contractions. They're the body's way of preparing itself to give birth. They can start weeks or even months before true labor begins."

"Basically false labor pains," Alice says.

I didn't know pains could be false.

"Wait, so, if you're having Braxton . . ."

"Hicks," her mom offers.

"Right. Then how can you tell when the real contractions start?"

"It feels very different. Braxton-Hicks contractions are uncomfortable, but most doctors don't call them false labor pains, because they're usually not painful. In a real contraction, the pain starts low, then rises like a wave. For some women their cervix may dilate. With Alice, I passed the mucus plug shortly after contractions began."

"Mom!"

"There's nothing shameful about labor, Alice."

"Does it hurt a lot?" I ask, even though I already know the answer. "Having a baby?"

"More than anything I have ever experienced."

Alice shifts in the front seat. Her mom just called her the most painful thing she's ever experienced.

I wonder if my mom would say the same.

All of a sudden, I'm careening forward as Dr. Phan slams on the brakes. She lets loose a rapid-fire string of Vietnamese that I suspect we'd get in trouble for repeating, then mom-arms Alice, an automatic reflex where a mom throws her arm out to the right to keep her kid from smashing into the dashboard. I call it the Marm.

As the car lunges to a stop, my seat belt throws me back, hard. But my heart isn't pounding.

"You okay?" Alice says, twisting around to check on me. Her expression is hard to read.

"Everybody's okay," says Dr. Phan, more of a statement than a question.

I crane my neck to look out the window—and then I see why Alice's mom stopped so abruptly.

A pack of kids zigzags across the busy street, waving their arms and yelling. I watch one boy hurl an object into oncoming traffic. An egg? A rock?

When he wheels around, I find myself staring at Thom Strong. There's something feral in his eyes.

"Reckless kids," Dr. Phan mutters, shaking her head. "What's gotten into them?"

Maybe it's not what's gotten into them. It's what's gotten out.

⊙

Alice's house is the nicest house I've ever seen in real life. She ushers me into a foyer with spotless marble floors, a glinting chandelier, and a gigantic painting of a black-haired girl in a long flowing white dress, her face obscured by a tapered white straw hat.

"I call this the vestibule," Alice says, gesturing around the foyer. "And I call her"—she nods toward the ghostly figure—"the vestighoul."

I giggle. "Well, she's wearing a very nice ghoulish dress."

"It's actually a tunic. See how it's split? It's called an áo dài, and you wear pants underneath. The nón lá—that's her hat—is made from palm leaves dried in the sun so they turn that silvery-white color. The leaves get ironed flat, sewn onto a conical bamboo frame, and then the nón lá is coated with rose petal oil to make it waterproof. Cool, right?"

I nod in wonder. I can't believe I only saw a dress and a straw hat.

Alice leads me down a narrow hallway past more expensive-looking paintings to a staircase flanked by two big blue urns.

"Nice urns," I say.

"Ah, so you've met my late uncles."

I choke. Alice erupts into laughter.

"I'm kidding, Zia! No ashes in there. Just rarefied air." She beckons. "C'mon, I'll show you my room."

Her *wing* is more like it. Alice has her own bathroom, a

library with a designated homework alcove, and a kitchen that's almost as big as our entire apartment. Everything is bright white, almost sterile. Which seems . . . wrong? When I think of Alice, I see sparkling colors, peacocks and mermaids and tangerines.

"It looks like a hospital." Alice sighs. "Occupational hazard of living with two doctors. My parents like everything to be clean. *Oppressively* clean."

Alice's bedroom is much more Alicious. Her bomber jackets hang from the wall in one long row, every color of the rainbow—and then some besides. In between the jackets, posters of famous comedians are pinned in place by funny buttons. For an extra dose of magic, fairy lights dangle from a large canopy bed in the center of the room.

I don't know what compels me to take a flying twisty leap onto the bed—but that's exactly what I do. I land on my back in an explosion of pillows, fairy lights swaying gently overhead.

"This room is amazing. This bed is amazing! I can't believe you sleep here every night."

"I'm very lucky," Alice says, in a tone that sounds practiced.

"What's it like having two doctor parents?"

"Like this." She gestures around the room. "I have my own private suite, and I see my parents twice a week."

"Oh. I didn't mean—"

"No, it's okay. I mean it when I say I'm lucky. They're very generous and buy me nice things."

She flops down on her back beside me.

"Can I tell you a secret?" Alice says.

I prop myself up on one elbow, securing my glasses before they slip down my nose. "I eat secrets for breakfast."

She props herself up, eyes meeting mine.

"I'd trade it all to sit at the kitchen table with my parents, just talking and eating chè trôi nước."

I wait, sensing she has more to say.

"My ông nội used to live with us. My grandfather from Vietnam. He watched me, since my parents were gone so much. He's the one who taught me how to make chè. You've never had it, right?"

I shake my head.

"Ông Nội had his own secret recipe, and he passed it down to my dad. There are like five billion steps. You fill sticky rice balls with mung bean paste and cook them in a pot, like soup. Once they rise to the top, you soak them in warm, sweet ginger syrup, drizzle them with velvety coconut cream, sprinkle a dash of toasted sesame seeds on top—and you've got the best dessert in the whole history of desserts."

"I can't wait to try it."

Alice doesn't respond right away. She shuts her eyes, then exhales slowly.

"I guess you'll have to," she says. "I've tried to make chè by myself, but it never comes out quite right." She pauses. "Ông Nội died last year."

I can feel Alice's sadness. It's almost palpable, a big ball of grief rising to the top of the pot.

"I'm sorry," I say, and mean it.

She sits all the way up.

"My mom found out she was pregnant the week after we lost my ông. She and my dad had been trying to have another baby for a while. Years, actually. So suddenly that became their whole focus. And like, I get it. They've been heartbroken every time it doesn't work out. And now they're so close. Of course they're terrified something will go wrong."

It takes me a minute to follow her train of thought.

Terrified. Right. Now I remember. I feel a thrum of pleasure that, thanks to the dictionary, the Phans won't ever have to feel terrified again.

Thoughtful, Alice plucks the gray hair band around her wrist.

"I used to practice my jokes on Ông Nội, because he always had time for me. I knew how to make him laugh. I want to make my parents laugh, too. They seriously need it! But they're just too worried about the baby, and too distracted to pay attention to anything or anyone else. They have literally no idea I want to be a stand-up comic."

"Wait, haven't you been staying after school for Story Club?"

"They think I'm meeting with my math tutor."

"Yikes."

"Yikes to the eleventh degree."

Alice's smile is back, and I'm glad to see it. There's something mischievous in her grin.

"My parents wanted me to stay at my old school, but I begged to go to Ryden this year. I argued that it offered a more diverse student body and broader extracurricular options." She shrugs. "Not a lie. My old school didn't even have a theater department, let alone Story Club."

I snort. "You came to Ryden for comedy?"

"Why is that funny?"

"It's just, in my experience, Ryden is more of a tragedy."

She laughs. "Welcome to junior high."

Alice waves a hand in front of her face, like she's clearing the words.

"Enough about me. The Story Jamboree is tomorrow after school. I don't want to force you into anything . . . but I really think you might enjoy it."

My chest puffs with pride. Alice thinks I might enjoy the thing *she* enjoys.

"I'm game to try."

"Really?" She brightens. "Cool!"

"So what do I do?"

"Just tell me a story."

My stomach is suddenly a bucket of nerves. I grope around my brain for a story that Alice will find interesting or impressive. She's giving me the floor, and I don't want to waste it.

"A story about what?" I ask.

"About anything. Something I don't know about you. Something real."

And, just like that, it comes to me. I know exactly what story to tell her. A story that's been brewing inside me for the past two years.

I tell Alice about the Wandering Summer.

kilarious |ki-ˈler-ē-əs|
adjective

1 marked by or causing extreme hilarity, followed by an emotional sucker punch to the gut: *Zia Angelis is totally kilarious*.

From English *hilarious*, "extremely funny" and *kill*, "put an end to."

I was nine when Mom declared a bankrupture, the kind of earthquake where all your money falls through the cracks. We put our stuff in storage and house-sat for a bunch of different families while they were off on their fancy summer vacations.

"Why don't we stay with Yiayia?" I remember asking. "She has a big house."

To which Mom replied, "We don't need a big house, Sunshine Girl. We only need each other."

She was right. Even without a home, I was happy. We stayed in one upstairs duplex where we could walk onto the downstairs unit's roof, and we'd bring our shared scoop of ice cream up there to watch the sunset. Another house had a family of silkworms living in a mulberry tree. Mom never missed an opportunity to make a special memory, so she surprised me one morning with mulberry sandwiches and an impromptu tea party.

Sometimes I'd invite Sasha and Jay over, and we'd embark on a Zashay adventure, scouring the house for secret doors or passageways, making up stories about the people who lived there and the lives they led.

I tell Alice how it was weird and confusing, waking up in so many strange beds, but also funny, living amid other people's stuff. How Mom and I would stumble across their secrets without meaning to. Like the time we were house-sitting for two newlyweds and opened a ton of kitchen drawers looking for a can opener . . . and found a Polaroid picture of them hiking buck naked. Mom blushed extra pink when I asked if that's why they called it a honey*moon*.

I try to make Alice understand how, in a summer of honeymoon pictures and mulberry sandwiches, my gerbil Gerber Baby was a fuzzy brown cuddlebug of happy. We didn't have Mouseimus yet, which was probably a good thing, seeing as how Mr. Mousie does *not* like riding in the car. But Baby didn't mind it. We carried his cage from house to house, and I was a responsible pet parent, cleaning out the old stinky cedar chips, chopping up carrots and lettuce, and letting Baby tickle my face with his squiggly pink nose.

And then I tell Alice about the day it all came to an end. Mom and I were pet-sitting for a family with an excitable black lab puppy. One night we went out for burgers, and while we were gone, the lab knocked the cage off the counter.

I was the one who found Baby. He was lying very still in a panicked trail of cedar chips. He didn't have a scratch on him, but his eyes were open wide. Mom said he died of fright.

I cried for hours. I didn't know it was possible to cry that much. Mom held me while I left a blubbery mess of tears and snot on her soft nubby sweater. At the time I couldn't imagine anything worse than losing Baby.

Little did I know.

It hurts, confessing all this to Alice. I haven't talked about Baby in a long time, not since the Shadoom erased everything that came before. The memory feels like a wound inside me: raw and red and not quite healed. My eyes fill with tears when I get to the part about finding him in the cedar chips, how still his little body was. No wriggling nose, no excited squeak to see me. He was just gone.

I was only nine, but even then I understood he wasn't coming back.

Alice listens attentively. She doesn't make any of the little sighs or *mm-hmm* noises people make. *Sympathy sounds*, Mom calls them.

When I'm finished, Alice stares at me. Still. Silent.

She hated it. I'm a terrible storyteller.

"Alice, say something."

"Wow. I just . . . wow."

"'Wow' as in, that was awful?"

"'Wow' as in, that was extraordinary."

Extraordinary (adjective): unusual, abnormal, outside the norm. I wince, remembering why I don't tell people about my life. Here I am, talking to a girl who was a complete stranger one week ago, sitting in her gorgeous mansion and confessing how my mom and I were basically homeless for a summer.

"I wish I'd had a summer like that," Alice says wistfully.

I blink. "Really? Why?"

"I don't mean losing Baby. That part sounds truly awful. But having all those adventures with your mom. And you tell the story so well. You do this thing . . . I don't even know how to describe it . . . where you're, like, really funny. Totally hilarious. And then right when you've got me laughing hysterically, you twist it around and say the saddest thing. You'll make some insight or observation, throw in a devastating little detail, and it's a knife to the heart. One second I'm sitting there grinning, and then the very next second you've killed me dead."

"I'm totally kilarious," I say, without missing a beat.

"See?" She eyes me up, impressed. "Genius."

I'm not always great at accepting compliments. Ask Jay. But the thing is, this time I know Alice is right. I *did* tell the story well. In some ways, talking about it—remembering the ache in my chest as my heart shattered into a million pieces— is like picking off a scab and making the blood flow again. But it's also a relief to say the words.

"I really did feel like I was right there with you," says Alice. "All the moving from place to place. Then walking into that house and finding Baby in the wood chips."

She snaps the red hair band around her wrist.

"I'm so sorry, Zia. That must have hurt so much."

Hearing Alice say that—I can't explain it, but it helps. While I was telling my story, the door to the dark room inside my chest started to creak open. But when Alice says those words, she strikes a match. Almost like, by listening to me talk about the pain, she helped heal it.

"I'll do the Story Jamboree."

Alice claps, gleeful.

"Best news ever! You don't have to sign up or anything—just come to the auditorium tomorrow after school. Parents are welcome, too."

"Including yours?" I ask wryly.

"Well . . . they would be." She grimaces. "If they knew it existed."

A sharp knock on the open door makes us both jump. "Girls?"

"Mom!" Alice says. "Way to scare us!"

I frown. *Way . . . to . . .*

The thought goes wonky in my head, and I don't finish it, because Dr. Phan Number One isn't alone.

There, in a flowy hippie skirt, looking painfully out of place in the Phans' antiseptic hallway with her Gravy hair in a messy bun, is *my* mom.

Something is wrong. I see it instantly in her expression. And she sees that I see it.

"It's okay, Z," she says, her voice eerily calm. "Everything's going to be okay. But it's time to come home."

I'm already reaching for my bag. The dictionary's hard edges press through the thin fabric.

"Did something happen? Where's Yiayia?"

"Yiayia's in the car. She's fine. But I was in the bedroom for a few minutes, and while I was there I guess she must have opened the front door and left it open, because by the time I came back out . . ."

She can't say the rest, so I say it for her.

"Mouseimus is gone."

jamboreasy peasy |ˈjam-bə-ˈrī-zē ˈpē-zē|
adjective

1 when a jamboree or other life event goes smoothly with no problems whatsoever: *Why can't things be jamboreasy peasy?*

Mom drives the Brownie home at normal speed, Yiayia dozing in the back seat. I want to feel angry at my grandmother for letting Mr. Mousie out, angry at Mom for being careless. I think I have a right to.

But I'm having a hard time feeling anything right now. I'm like a computer running diagnostic tests, drilling Mom on the *w*'s: Where, When, Why, and What Was She Thinking.

"How long did you leave Yiayia alone?"

"Only a few minutes."

"Long enough for her to open the door. Of course Mouseimus seized the opportunity—you know he's got kitty wanderlust."

Mr. Mousie is always gazing longingly out the window or darting through our ankles to run outside. The irony is that he's an indoor cat through and through: lazy, spoiled, and completely ill prepared for surviving the wild. The coyotes that roam our neighborhood would love nothing more than a nice house cat snack.

"I'm sorry," Mom mumbles, like I'm the mom and she's in trouble. Which is irritating.

Once we're parked outside the apartment, we leave Yiayia sleeping in the car and take opposite sides of the street, calling, "Mousie! Mousie!" We try the next block over, then the next. As dusk falls, moonlight melts the gray pavement into silver glitter—and makes it easier to check under bushes and parked cars.

"We'll find him," Mom says, but her voice is Sure Hope So, not For Sure.

For the first time since leaving the Phans, I feel something other than cold logic. The thought of losing Mr. Mousie floods my chest with a deep, painful ache. Mom brought Mouseimus home from the shelter the day after Baby died. My face was still gummy with tears, but as soon as I saw that fat little tabby, the tears stopped.

I can't imagine life without Mr. Mousie. I don't want to.

I'm about to ask for a Lightning Bug when Mom says, "Shh. Do you hear that?"

I do hear it. A low, throaty growl.

Mom takes my hand, and together we walk down the driveway of a brown bungalow. The sound gets louder as a motion-sensor light clicks on.

And then I see the source of the growl.

Two orange marmalade cats are curled in front of the garage. We've seen them around the neighborhood, though I don't think they belong to anyone. Sometimes Mom puts out a dish of sweet milk for them to lap up.

Lying beside the strays is Mouseimus.

All the pent-up air rushes out of me. The Mouseimus-shaped nook in my heart fills to the brim.

But none of these cats are the ones growling. Nope.

That would be the mountain lion.

I didn't know we had mountain lions around these parts. Not for a thousand miles. Turns out I was wrong, and Yiayia was right.

Mr. Brockmeier says mountain lions are also called pumas, like the shoe but with sharper teeth. And while pumas are technically cats, this one is four times bigger than Mr. Mousie— and probably ten times as strong.

Mr. Brockmeier says mountain lions are predators. Judging by Mr. Puma's ravenous growl and coiled leg muscles, I'd wager he's ready to spring on his prey.

We are seconds away from a pumassacre. I can see tomorrow's headline: "Local Dance Teacher and Weirdling Daughter Eaten by Mountain Lion While Trying to Save Three Small Cats." If by some miracle I survive, *this* is the story I should tell at the Jamboree.

But here's where it gets weird.

The three small cats aren't bothered in the slightest. No arched backs, no bared teeth, no poofed tails. Mouseimus swats lazily at a blade of grass. One of the strays hacks up a hairball.

"Shoo!" Mom has found an old broom in the bungalow's backyard. She brandishes it like a not-very-pointy sword. "Go!"

The puma regards her with curiosity, but he doesn't run. Just watches.

I squeeze my brain folds together. There's a word—a feeling—I can't quite grasp. The cats aren't . . .

Afraid. The word snaps into focus. The cats aren't afraid of the mountain lion . . . and the mountain lion isn't afraid of us.

But he's still hungry.

Hungry for a nice mom snack.

"Uh, Mom?"

"It's okay, Sunshine Girl." She smiles brightly, which under the circumstances makes her look slightly deranged. "I'll just scoop up Mr. Mousie and we can head on home."

Something clicks. I've spent all day counting the hours until fear is gone completely. For me it's still a flickering light bulb.

For Mom, that bulb has burned all the way out.

"Come here, kitty boy!" she says to Mr. Mousie, who moves not an inch. Mom takes a perilous step forward.

"*Mom.*"

I look from her to the mountain lion to Mouseimus, my gaze pinging between prey, predator, prey. Then Mr. Mousie, with a showstopping yawn, rolls onto his back, exposing his fluffy white tummy for all the world to see.

The feeling that wells up inside me isn't fear. It's worse. It is the bone-deep knowledge of what my life would be like, not just without Mouseimus, but without Mom. The black hole it would leave inside me that nothing would ever fill.

An idea ignites in my brain.

"*Do not*," I growl at Mom, in a tone so deep it surprises us both. "*Move. A. Muscle.*"

I sprint all three blocks back to the car on a burst of adrenaline. I'm clenching my fists, as if I could hold onto the memory of fear by brute force. If fear will help me run faster, I have to marshal every ounce I have left.

⊙

In the Brownie, I tear the *C. Scuro Dictionary* out of my bag and fly to M, shaking the matáki eraser into my hand.

My eyes bulge out of their sockets.

What happened to the rest of the eraser?

The matáki eye is half the size it was the last time I held it. The outer ring of electric blue is gone, as is most of the pale blue inside it.

Have I really used that much? I swear it wasn't this tiny before I erased FEAR. But maybe erasing big words takes a bigger chunk out of the eraser? That makes sense, seeing as how FEAR had a big fat word family, with FEARFUL and FEARSOME and FEARSTRUCK all vying loudly for attention. Kind of like a big Greek family where everyone's clamoring to be front and center.

That's how the Greek families are on TV, anyway. Ours is small and quiet.

All the more reason I have to do everything in my power to save it.

I riffle swiftly from MA to MO. Desperate times call for desperate erasures.

mountain lion |ˈmaunt-ən ˈlī-ən|
noun

1 a large, powerful tawny-brown cat: *You didn't know you had mountain lions around these parts.*

I feel a pang. Do I really want to erase all mountain lions? It doesn't seem fair. And there's another question gnawing at me, a creeping awareness that Mouseimus, too, is a large tawny-brown cat, just not a particularly powerful one. What if something misfires and by erasing mountain lions, I erase Mr. Mousie?

My hand hovers over the page.

And then, miraculously, I am spared. Mom strolls up the sidewalk. Uneaten, with a rotund tabby cat tucked under one arm.

Tumbling out of the Brownie, I slam the door behind me. "Mom!"

I take a running leap and throw my arms around her neck.

"Choking!" she croaks. "Choking." I loosen my grip. She

unlatches my hands the rest of the way, then hands Mouseimus to me like a sack of cat-atoes.

"Everything's okay, Sunshine Girl. I told you it would be! All cats are fine, including the big one. He's ambling back home, wherever that is."

"But how did you—"

"I gave him a good whack on the behind." She laughs. "What a day it's been! I danced for hours, quit my jobs, *and* faced down a mountain lion."

I swallow hot air. "You did what?"

"I faced down a—"

"Before that."

She stretches her arms overhead. "Didn't I tell you? I quit the dance studio and The Sweet Potato. I can't remember the last time I felt so free."

"But food isn't free. Rent isn't free."

Usually I wouldn't say those things out loud. But today *I* feel free, too.

Mom rolls her eyes.

"Don't be such a pain, Z! We'll figure it out. We always do."

I'm about to inform her *she's* the one being a pain, when an agonizing scream stops me cold.

Mom's head jerks toward the car. "Where's your yiayia?"

"She was . . ."

Only then do I realize she wasn't in the car just now. She

must have woken up and wandered off while Mom and I were searching.

How could I be so careless?

"Mom, I'm . . ."

It doesn't matter what I am. My words are engulfed by Yiayia's screams.

⊙

My grandmother is bent over the kitchen stove. Hot blue flames crackle around the front burner. She cradles her right hand to her chest.

Seared into her palm is a red spiral. The brightest, shiniest, angriest red I have ever seen.

"Mana mou," Mom says softly. "What have you done?"

And Yiayia begins to cry.

idea |ī-ˈdē-ə|

noun

    1 something imagined or pictured in the mind

    2 a concept, notion, or mental impression: *Where is the boundary between a word and the idea behind it?*

The emergency room is full of people hurting.

A baby girl screams bloody murder as her parents pass her back and forth, one jiggling her gently while the other rubs her back. Across the room, a stocky guy clutches a bloody dish towel around his hand. Beside us, a little boy hangs on to his mom's arm, struggling to breathe. He keeps clawing at his throat like there's something lodged inside that he can't get out.

"It's all right," his mother says. "You're going to be all right." But I can see how hard she's trying not to cry.

And then there's Yiayia.

I can't stop staring at her hand. The entire stove coil is scorched viciously into her palm. Skin stretched and shiny, already blistering like a sinister pink balloon.

"It looks like a maze, Yiayia," I say, hoping to distract her. "Or a labyrinth."

Mom pats her arm. "Hear that, Mana? You gave yourself a labyrinth. How very Greek of you."

We're both trying to get her mind off the pain, but it doesn't work. She hasn't stopped crying since we arrived. That was hours ago.

"I lose so much," Yiayia murmurs, rocking slightly. "My attic of artifacts. My odds. I lose my eggs and baskets." She strings together thoughts I can't quite follow. "I try to take, want to take. I could not see it. Something, then no thing. But my hand. So many tears, gone."

"I know, Mana." Mom says, stroking the papery skin of her arm. She's much better at deciphering Yiayia-speak than I am. "I know."

Mom's forehead crease is deeper than I've ever seen it. There are lines around her eyes, too, tiny bolts of lightning.

I feel a tight, sinking sensation in my belly. Every time I look at Yiayia's burn, the sink drops lower.

Because I know, more surely than I have ever known anything, that this is my fault.

When a nurse finally comes to get us, she leads us through the double doors and into another smaller waiting room. This one is empty. I sit motionless in a hard plastic chair with a scooped-out butt until a different nurse comes to take Mom and Yiayia away.

I want to push aside the horrible, heavy knowledge of what I've done. But I can't escape it. The second we walked into the hospital, I could smell it in the waiting room. It's floating in the air. Blaring in the hard fluorescent lights. Caked into the chairs.

FEAR.

It sears itself onto my retinas in a brilliant blaze of glory, the way a star burns brightest right before it's snuffed out forever. A supernova of fear. I don't know how long I can hold

147

on to it. I already feel those four letters seeping through the porous lobes of my brain as I begin to forget.

But I can't let it slip away. I was wrong. It turns out we need fear. It tells us when we're in danger. It fuels our reflexes. Fear protects silly little cats from hungry big ones. It keeps kids from throwing rocks at oncoming traffic and grandmothers from touching hot stoves.

Maybe I can fix this. Before it's too late.

I heave my backpack onto my lap. I'm not at all surprised when the C. *Scuro Dictionary* opens right to FE. Between FEALTY and FEASIBLE, a long white column stares up at me.

The pages begin to move. They riffle wildly from FE to AF to SC to TE, and I see other empty spaces, my mind quickly filling in the blanks.

AFRAID.

SCARED.

TERRIFIED.

No wonder the eraser is shrinking so fast. I erased FEAR's immediate word family, but the dictionary took the liberty of hunting down all its synonyms and related words. Sentence by sentence, letter by letter, the C. *Scuro Dictionary: 13th Edition* has been erasing itself.

I muscle my way back to where FEAR should be, which isn't easy—the dictionary is freakishly strong. Sweat stings the back of my neck. With one hand I pry the pages open, plunging my other hand deep into my backpack.

My fingers close around a pen.

It's now or never. I hold the pen to the paper like a knife to a throat . . . and try to write FEAR back into the dictionary.

I get as far as *f* before my hand clenches, unable to move.

Beneath me, the ink shivers to life.

The *f* twists out of reach. Whirling, birling, it sprouts two perfect wings, lifts off the barren white field and soars across the page to FEATHER, where it bursts into a brilliant peacock fan. It floats higher, sprouts a turkey wattle, and waddles onto a plate. Nearby letters contort into more plates, platters, goblets, bowls of sugared grapes. I can almost hear the clang of cutlery.

The FEAST splinters like glass. Ink twists and trembles, swirling into longer, smoother lines. A woman appears, with a cumulus poof of white hair and a thermometer in her mouth. 104.1 DEGREES, it reads. FEBRILE: having or showing symptoms of a fever.

It dawns on me, slowly, that there is no longer a blank column. While the dictionary was playing tricks, the definitions and etymologies and example sentences were jostling one another, some letters growing, some letters shrinking. Now, as the ink stills, the page has revised itself.

The word I erased, then tried to write back in? Every trace of it has vanished. There are no gaps, no empty spaces. Almost like the word was never there at all.

Maybe it wasn't. In my own mind, the light bulb goes dark and silent. The star dies.

Somehow I know that, this time, the word isn't coming back.

☉

I must doze off, because when I open my eyes, Yiayia is sitting in the scooped-butt chair beside me. She stares at her hand, now bandaged in stiff white gauze.

Then she fixes me with a penetrating look.

"You are strong, paidaki mou," she says quietly. "More strong than your yiayia."

I wish so much that that were true.

Mom stands in the doorway, speaking quietly with an Asian doctor in a white coat.

"You'll need to clean and dress the wound twice daily," he's saying, "so it doesn't get infected. Soap and water is fine. If she starts to show symptoms of a fever, I want to see her back here immediately."

"Will the pain be better tomorrow?"

"Burns tend to be worse the second day, once the adrenaline fades. I would give her ibuprofen when you get home tonight, then every four to six hours to help with the pain."

Mom notices I'm awake.

"Zia." She motions me over. "This is Dr. Phan. Thanks to him, your grandmother is all patched up."

Dr. Phan is tall and broad shouldered, with dark round

glasses the same shape as mine. His face is both kind and curious in a way that's instantly familiar.

"You're Dr. Phan Number Two."

"Beg pardon?"

"You're Alice's dad, aren't you?"

He blinks in surprise. "I am. Are you two friends?"

I nod. "I was at your house earlier. You have very nice wall art."

He smiles. "Thank you, Zia."

"You were supposed to pick us up after school so we could make sticky rice balls." Mom shoots me a Stop-Talking-Right-Now glare, but I don't stop. "Alice was really looking forward to it."

Dr. Phan's smile stays stuck to his face, but his eyes stop smiling. He clears his throat.

"I'm sorry we didn't get to do that. Some other time."

"It's kilarious seeing you here," I say, instantly regretting my word choice.

No one is laughing much at all.

⊙

We walk through the main waiting room on our way out. New faces have replaced the old ones, including a boy with his arm in a hard white cast.

Thom Strong.

My first thought—and I'm not proud to admit it—is, *Serves him right.* When you charge across streets and chuck rocks at drivers, you're just asking for a broken bone.

But no. Thom isn't here for that. He already *has* a cast.

The reason he's in the emergency room is his mom.

She's hunched over in a chair, holding an ice pack to her face. A dark purple bruise blooms around her right eye. The color is familiar: It matches the purple smudge on Thom's wrist I saw at lunch today. The one he was so eager to cover up.

Someone did this to her. Someone a lot bigger than her son.

Thom stares me down, daring me to speak.

And then I understand. When I erased the thing I erased, my mom faced down a mountain lion and quit her jobs. Thom's dad did something much worse.

Thom turns away from me, placing his good hand on his mom's shoulder. But not before I see twelve years of pain and lies and secrets leaking from his eyes.

hurt |ˈhert|
verb

1 to inflict with physical pain or bodily injury; to wound: *Someone hurt Thom.*

2 to do substantial or material harm; to damage: *Something hurt Yiayia.*

3 to feel emotional pain, suffering, or anguish: *Zia hurts.*

We don't talk on the drive back from the hospital. There isn't much to say. When we get home, Mom feeds Yiayia a painkiller and tucks her into bed. Then she pulls a step stool over to our closet.

"Mom?"

She doesn't answer.

"Mom? Are you mad at me?"

Balanced on the step stool, she lifts a shoebox off the top shelf.

I'm not supposed to know what's inside, but I do. One time when I was supposed to be asleep, I saw Mom take it out. A few days later, when she was late coming home from work, I took the shoebox out myself.

What I found were photographs of Mom when she was young. Not the ones I'd seen on Yiayia's staircase wall—those were mostly of kid Mom, with one lone shot of teenaged Mom in her ruby red leotard. In the shoebox pictures, she's in high school, then college, dancing, laughing, hanging out with friends. She looked happy in a way I'd never seen her. I couldn't shake the feeling that the reason she looked different now was *me*.

But tonight Mom doesn't care if I see. She closes the closet door with her foot, sealing in my glow-in-the-dark stars, and carries the shoebox to the living room, where she curls up with it on the couch.

I follow, then stop a few feet away, suddenly uncertain.

"Can I look, too?"

She doesn't respond. Just hands me a picture of a girl with Gravy black hair and a big toothy smile. I don't remember seeing this one before.

"That's your yiayia."

"*That's* Yiayia?" I squint, trying to imagine how, if you ironed out Old Yiayia's wrinkles, Young Yiayia would shine through.

"She looks happy," I say.

"She does, doesn't she?" Mom taps the photograph lightly. "I never really saw her like that. She was sad a lot when I was a kid. She sort of . . . withdrew into herself. I think she missed her family."

"You *are* her family."

"I meant her family in Greece. She never talked about them. It used to make me so mad! I felt like she was hiding my own history from me. But I never told her I was angry, because I didn't want to hurt her feelings. I spent so many years as a kid wishing my mom would tell me stories."

I know what Mom means. Other than the one magical afternoon in the Attifact, Yiayia has never told me stories, either.

Mom pats the couch beside her. Grateful, I slide onto the cushion.

"You know how the doctors were running all those tests?" she says. "They believe Yiayia has dementia."

"What's dementia?"

"The short answer is that it's a disease that can make people forget things. At some point, she'll forget even the simplest things."

"Like how you shouldn't put your hand on a hot stove."

"Exactly like that."

"Will Yiayia forget us?" I ask.

Mom's shoulders droop. "I'm not going to lie to you. She might."

Mom sifts through more photographs. She stops at one, and her breathing changes. She's very quiet.

Finally, she says, "This is your pappoúli."

She hands me a square photograph of a man with kind eyes and a bushy black mustache.

"I know this picture!" I balance it tenderly on my knee. "Yiayia had the same one on her wall. But then one day it wasn't there anymore."

Mom smiles. The kind of smile that hurts to look at—and probably hurts to give.

"I'm sure it made her sad to see it. Mana was never any good at feeling sad."

It's a curious thing to say, because I've never thought of people being *good* or *bad* at feelings.

"I know I never talk about your pappoúli," Mom says. "He passed away in a car accident before you were born. He would have adored you."

I feel my whole body tilt forward. This is more than she's ever said about my grandfather. I knew he died, but I didn't know how. The thought that my pappoúli would adore me makes me warm all the way down to my toes.

"What was he like?" I ask.

"Gentle. Funny. He always knew how to make me laugh. And he could be so silly! You remind me of him sometimes."

"I'm sillarious," I quip, but she doesn't seem to notice.

"He's the one who named our dog Tzatziki. Mana thought it was absurd, but Baba and I died laughing. He was a great storyteller. His stories made me feel all the things."

Mom's face is softer now. Soaked in the memory.

I feel a warm flush of hope. If my grandfather's stories made Mom feel all the things, maybe I can stir up the same magic at the Story Jamboree tomorrow. What if a story is the best possible gift I could give her?

"Your pappoúlis and yiayia were a funny match in so many ways," she says. "But he sure did love her. And he loved me, too. To the stars and back."

"Do you miss him?" I ask.

"Every day."

The raw pain in her voice ripples through me. I can't believe she's never told me this. That she's been sitting with this heartache, alone, all these years.

She takes the photograph gently from my hand. Shakes her head.

"When did I become my mana? Sometimes I think the women in our family are cursed. We carry our grief silently inside us, and it's such a heavy burden. All these years I haven't talked about my baba, because the memories were just too painful. But I think that was a mistake. I think *not* talking about him hurts even worse."

A shadow passes over her face. She slides my pappoúli back into the pile. With one hand, she frees her hair from the bun, and it tumbles down her shoulders in long, loose waves. She sifts through more photographs, faster this time, and hands me a new one.

"This is from my last college dance recital. I was twenty-two."

It's one of the pictures I found in the shoebox before. She looks gorgeous, with glitter streaked over both cheeks. Her black hair is chopped into a cute shiny bob and she's wearing a leopard-print leotard and bright red ballet slippers with ribbons laced all the way up her calves.

"I was pregnant with you when this picture was taken. I had no idea." She shakes her head. "Look at me! I'm just a kid myself."

The words sound strange, like they're not really meant for me. Is she sad? Angry? Disappointed? Disappointed in me or in herself?

"Mom?"

I place my hand on her arm, hoping to beam her some sunshine.

It backfires.

My fingertips stick like frostbite. The room around me starts to go dark.

No. Not now. Not here.

But it *is* here, and it *is* now. I feel like a Zia-shaped kitchen sponge, soaking up Mom's feelings drop by drop. Inside my chest, the Shadoom paces the room. Thirsty.

"Mom?" I whisper. "Can I have a Lightning Bug?"

She exhales. A long, heavy breath.

"Sweet Zia. I love you to the stars and back. But I've got nothing for you right now. I don't even have anything for myself."

I love you, but.

Not *I love you,* and. *I love you,* but.

Mom drops her head into her hands.

"I'm so tired," she moans. "Years and years of working all these jobs to make ends meet. And now I'm supposed to take care of my mother, too? My feet are killing me. My back is killing me."

"I don't want you to hurt."

"It doesn't matter what you want, Zia. Being a mom hurts. Being *alive* hurts."

She says something else, but I don't hear it.

Being a mom hurts.

She might as well have said, *Being* your *mom hurts.*

The words hang in the air between us. They swarm the dark room inside me, burrowing into the walls. I hear Dr. Phan Number One in the car, talking about giving birth to Alice.

The most painful thing she has ever experienced.

What if Mom thinks that, too? And what if the pain didn't stop the day I was born? What if the reason she looks happy and carefree in those photographs is because I've been hurting her ever since?

Mom lifts her head. Her eyes refocus on me. She reaches out to touch my cheek.

"Let's go to bed, Sunshine Girl. Everything will look sunnier in the morning."

But all I see inside of me is rain.

☉

I lie awake for hours. Years. Eons. The lenses of my glasses keep smudging, until I remember I'm not actually wearing my glasses. Those are just my eyes, smudgy with tears.

In her bed across the room, Yiayia whispers strange incantations to herself. They're mostly in Greek, but even the ones in English don't make sense. *Grab an egg and shave it. You made it a sea. I ate the world to find you.* Then something about the Attifact. They sound more and more like the feverish ravings of a madwoman, until finally I get up and take her temperature to make sure she isn't febrile.

She isn't. But she is definitely in pain. She whimpers, tossing and turning, unable to get comfortable. Every time she rolls onto her burned hand she cries out.

Yiayia hurts because of me.

Mom hurts because of me.

Thom, Thom's mom, that little baby in the ER: they all hurt because of me.

And what I'm finally beginning to understand is: *I* hurt because of me. The unnamable thing inside me, this ugly broken thing, isn't going away. It was only a matter of time until the Shadoom came for me. That's just the way I am.

Sometimes I look at other kids and think, *Lucky them.* They're made of puppies and pancakes. Meanwhile I'm a modern twist on that other Greek, King Midas, who turned everything he touched into gold. Only instead of gold, everything I touch turns to pain.

I can erase pain.

Boom.

Cue lightning bolt and violin crescendo.

The voice in my head is quick to argue. *Are you sure that's a good idea? Look what happened last time.*

The voice isn't wrong. I don't even remember what word I

erased, but I know erasing it was a mistake: it kept good people from doing dangerous things and bad people from doing horrible things.

But pain? Pain is what happens *after*. It comes in different shapes: physical, emotional, braineal. I might not be able to prevent all the horrible and dangerous things . . . but I can make sure they don't hurt the people I care about.

As for me?

The Shadoom eats pain for breakfast. Without pain, it will never survive.

Quietly I pull the C. *Scuro Dictionary* out of my bag. I thumb through the pages, stopping at PAGE ☉ PALACE. There, in the left column, is PAIN. Nine definitions, eighteen related words, and a dizzyingly long list of synonyms: ACHE. AGONY. ANGUISH. GRIEF. HEARTACHE.

The ink begins to run and trickle. I press down hard with the eraser, chasing every stream. I don't want the dictionary to entertain me with a lively, illustrated demonstration of all the different types of pain.

I just want to erase it.

GAD |ˈgad|
acronym: Generalized Anxiety Disorder

ɪ an anxiety disorder characterized by excessive,
uncontrollable, and often irrational   .

I know from the moment I wake up. My chest doesn't hurt. My brain doesn't hurt.

There is no HURT. Which means there is no Shadoom.

There also isn't much eraser. I erased all the synonyms of PAIN myself, because I didn't trust the *C. Scuro Dictionary* to do it for me.

Sitting up in bed, I scrutinize the babáki. My eyebrows scrunch. I didn't think I had used *that* much. The inner white ring of the matáki eye is gone, leaving nothing but the black pupil. How is it disappearing so fast?

I can squeeze out one more erasure, maybe. Something small.

That's okay. Once PAIN has completely dissolved, including the idea behind it, there won't be any other big stuff I need to erase.

I stroll into the kitchen, sunny as the day I was born.

"Good morning, Z!" Mom says chipfully. That's when you're chipper and cheerful at the same time. She's wearing red ballet slippers with ribbons laced up her calves—shoes I didn't know she still owned—and her Sweet Potato apron.

A wisp of sense memory blows through me. Something about that apron. Then it's gone.

"Hot spanakopita," Mom announces, "fresh out of the oven!"

"Spanakopita for breakfast?"

"That's what I said, too. But your yiayia insisted."

She flicks a hand toward my grandmother, who is standing a little too close to the stove.

"I thought she wasn't supposed to be in the kitchen."

"I thought you weren't supposed to be so bossy," Mom snaps, in a tone that surprises me. I study her face, trying to get a read on her mood. I know we had a conversation last night on the sofa. What did we talk about? My brain feels echoey, like there's more space inside than usual. Which is odd, because in order for there to be echoes, there has to be something there first.

"With farts you cannot dye eggs," Yiayia says.

Mom cocks her head to one side. "I guess," she says slowly, "that is technically true."

She laughs. I laugh, too, relieved. But the air doesn't quite feel right between us.

Then again, from the sour look on Yiayia's face, maybe it's the air between *them* that's not right.

"I woke up today feeling like a million bucks," Mom says. "I've been dancing around the apartment all morning. My body feels . . . different?" She laughs again. "I fell out of a pirouette and it didn't even hurt. I'm twenty-two again! Invincible."

I stare at her ankle—and gasp. It's so swollen it looks like a butternut squash. Butternut squankle.

Yiayia is staring at Mom's squankle, too.

"Paidaki mou," she says. "I can take this."

"No, Mana," Mom says flatly.

"In our family, we fight many tears. You must not feel—"

"No."

I feel like they're having a silent conversation underneath the words they're actually saying.

Yiayia tries again. "If you would only take—"

"I said NO! I'm *fine*. I can live with it." Mom's voice is suddenly fierce. "Has it ever occurred to you that maybe you shouldn't have taught me to keep everything locked up inside? To bury whatever I'm feeling?"

"I want home!" Yiayia says miserably. "I want attic."

I wait for Mom to tell her all the reasons she can't go to the Attifact, or to her house, or anywhere she might hurt herself. But Mom shrugs.

"Sure. Go."

I frown. "Wait, I thought—"

"What is this?" My grandmother starts picking furiously at the white gauze swathing her burn. "I can take away."

"No, no, no, Yiayia!" I rush toward her. "You have to keep the bandage on."

"I do not need." She looks at me, pleading. "You can take. Please take for me."

"Can you just keep it on, please?" I glance at Mom for backup. "Remember what Dr. Phan said?"

"Dunno." Mom shrugs. "Something about fever?"

Exasperated, I gesture toward the bottle of ibuprofen

that's still out from last night. "You're supposed to give her a painkiller every four to six hours."

"A what?"

"A . . ." There's the brain echo again. I clear my throat. "A . . . killer?"

No. That can't be right.

Mom snorts with laughter.

"Pretty sure I'm not supposed to give your yiayia a killer every four to six hours. Though sometimes I wonder!" She tosses a few puffy spanakopitas onto a plate. "Éla! Breakfast is served."

I reach for the plate, bemused. When I erased my first Big-Deal word, it took all day for it to completely erode. But it's happening faster now. The Big-Deal word I erased last night was still in my brain a few minutes ago when I came into the kitchen. Now it's gone.

I reassess Mom's swollen ankle. I mean, as long as it's not bothering her . . .

"It's Fri-Yay, Sunshine Girl!" she says, chipful once again. "You don't have to go to school today. You and I can play hooky."

I have to admit, playing hooky with Mom sounds fun. Then I remember the Jamboree.

"As long as I'm back at school this afternoon. I'm perform-ing at this story thing with Alice."

"Ooh, that sounds fun. What kind of story thing?"

"You basically just tell a story to the audience. You and Yiayia are invited." I take a breath. "In fact, I'm hoping you'll come."

"Hear that, Mana?" Mom's grin is somehow sharp. "Some people actually *want* to tell stories to their families!"

She wheels back around.

"What story are you going to tell, Z?"

"You'll have to wait and see."

I want it to be a surprise. No one knows the story of the Wandering Summer as well as Mom. If I tell it well, I'll be like my pappoúli, telling her stories that make her feel all the things.

Mom has spent so much time and energy giving me Lightning Bugs.

It's time I give one to her.

When we get to Ryden that afternoon, I'm walking on air. It's been a dream day with Mom—ice cream at What's the Scoop?, picnic in the park, even a cat movie. I don't know why I've been avoiding cat movies this year. Give me all the cats in all the movies, please.

Alice is waiting outside the school auditorium.

"There you are, Z!" Her whole face lights up. "I was afraid you weren't coming."

I blink. She waves at Mom and Yiayia, which is my cue to launch into a round of introductions.

"I heard you all had a run-in with my dad at the ER last night," Alice says. "I'm so sorry." She nods toward Yiayia's arm. "How's the pain? Burns are always worse the second day."

We all stare at Alice. I sneak a glance at Mom, who looks as confused as I am. What is Alice asking, exactly?

After a long beat, Yiayia says cryptically, "The many words are poor." All day she's been muttering strange things to herself, casting suspicious looks in my direction as she trailed Mom and me betrudgingly. That's when you trudge begrudgingly.

If Alice thinks this is a strange thing to say, she doesn't show it.

"Right this way," she says, ushering Mom and Yiayia into the auditorium. "We'll get you settled with the other distinguished theater patrons." By which she means two dozen beaming moms and one awkward dad thumbing through his iPhone.

"Zia is going to knock your socks off," Alice promises.

My heart skips half a beat when she takes my hand and leads me backstage.

☉

If anyone is a Sock Knocker, it's Alice.

I stand in the wings, watching as she steps into the

spotlight. I've heard the expression "takes the stage," but I've never fully understood it until Alice claims the microphone like an astronaut claiming the moon.

She's brilliant. Witty and sharp and one hundred percent real. Alice is humble without being self-deprecating, and she delivers razor-sharp social commentary that *slays*. But she never accuses or attacks her audience. She treats them like they're old friends in on the joke.

They love her. *I* love her. It's impossible not to.

Five minutes later, set completed, Alice strolls offstage to the sound of raucous applause.

The new girl in sixth grade has wowed us all.

"Well?" she asks between chugs of water. Her cheeks are flushed. "How was I?"

"Are you kidding? That was outstandingly Alicious. I already started your official fan club. We're the Phan Fans."

Alice cackles. I love when she cackles.

Then her grin wobbles. She twangs her violet hair band. "I wish my parents were here. I think they would have laughed."

"But they don't even know you're in Story Club."

"Yeah, I know. But still." The light in Alice's eyes switches off. "They're too busy with work and baby stuff anyway. They wouldn't have come, even if I'd asked."

A stagehand motions us to be quiet. She points at me and mouths, *You're up next.*

"You sure this is a good idea?" I whisper to Alice, my

glasses slipping down my nose. "My story's not *ha-ha* funny. It's actually kind of sad."

Alice holds my gaze. Then, gently, she lifts my glasses off my face. With her soft cotton sleeve, she buffs the rims until the sparkly suns turn gold. The gesture is so sweet, so unexpected, I don't know what to say.

She hooks the glasses carefully over my ears. Gives my arm a squeeze.

"Zia Angelis, you do kilarious better than anyone I know."

⊙

But Alice is wrong.

I'm not kilarious. I'm not anything.

Because the words don't come.

I've heard of performers "choking" onstage—I just never took it literally. Everything I want to say is lodged in my throat like a chunk of carrot. All the raw feeling that flowed out of me when I was telling Alice the story of Gerber Baby and the Wandering Summer?

Poof! Gone.

Mom leans forward in her seat so far she's at risk of face-planting onto the stage. I know she wants me to do well. So does Alice—in my periphery I see her in the wings, frantically snapping the elastic hair bands around her wrist.

You can do this! She flashes me a thumbs-up.

But it's useless. I know the word now, the one I erased. I know it because I feel the shape of it inside me, without any of the color or the texture or the weight.

Here's the thing about my story: It hurts. Hurts to tell, hurts to remember, hurts that I actually lived it. When I told it to Alice, it felt like I'd finally found a way to shed light on the pain by finding the humor inside it.

But now, standing onstage, I don't feel any pain. And without pain, there's nothing to shine the light on. There's no story to tell.

My face burns with humiliation. Why is it that when I finally find a way to make things better, they only get worse? It's so unfair. Words are my superpower. Despite all the ways I'm made wrong, they're the one thing I get right.

And now I don't have words, either.

The auditorium has gone so still I can't help but think of Baby lying on the cedar chips. The audience is dead silent as I exit the stage.

forget |fər-ˈget|
verb

   1 to put out of one's mind: *Forget about it.*
   2 to stop thinking or caring about something or someone: *She has forgotten me.*

I flee. Straight to the girls' restroom, gripping my backpack to my chest. Tears scalding my cheeks. I'll erase *jamborees* or *stories* or *humiliation*.

Maybe it'd just be easier to erase myself.

But no sooner have I ripped the *C. Scuro Dictionary* out of my bag than the restroom door swings open.

"Zia?"

Immediately I recognize my mistake. Of course she'd come here first. I shut my eyes tight, willing her to disappear.

"I see you," Alice says. "There under the stall."

Exactly what she said the day we met. Our Greet-Cute.

Only it doesn't feel so cute now.

I'm mad at Alice for dragging me to the Story Jamboree. Mad that she was amazing and I embarrassed myself. Mad that Alice Phan, apparently my only friend left in the universe, is about to see the *real* me: pathetic, tear-smudged, broken.

I bang open the stall door with my foot.

"What do you want, Alice?"

She takes a step back. "I just . . . I thought . . ." She hesitates, then crouches so we're at eye level. "Are you okay?"

"Do I *look* okay?"

I don't like the feelings roiling inside me. They're rough and jagged and impossible to name. Alice reaches for my hand, but I yank it out of reach. Her fingers come to rest on her three hair bands instead.

"Why do you wear those?" I spit. "News flash: hair bands are for hair."

I know I'm being mean, but I don't care. The last thing I want is Alice's pity.

"I'm sorry," she murmurs. "I shouldn't have pushed you to do the Jamboree. I guess I thought, maybe . . . it'd be something fun we could do together. Just hearing you tell your story was fun. I loved having you over to my house."

"You mean your palace."

She inhales sharply. "How did you know about that?"

Off my blank stare, she says, "I never invited anyone from my old school over to my house. Not once. But somehow it got out that both my parents were doctors, and they called me—"

"Palace Alice?" She nods. I shrug, even though it doesn't feel shruggish. But I'm in too deep to stop now. "They weren't wrong."

She presses her hand over her heart, like she's protecting it.

"That hurts, Z. That really hurts."

I feel like there are holes in her sentences. They don't fit together in my head. What is *hurt*, anyway?

"What are you even saying, Alice? Do you use big words to make people think you're cool?"

Her voice is pea-sized. "I thought you liked that I use big words."

"Half the time I don't even understand you. And I seriously doubt you understand me."

"I'm trying to!"

"Let me help you. While you're complaining about living in a palace, I share a one-bedroom apartment with my mom and grandma. I can't have chicken fingers in the cafeteria because I'm on Reduced Lunch. And I don't eat in a bathroom stall because it's *cool*. I do it because there's a room of shadows in my chest, and every time I try to make it go away, it only . . ."

The rest jams in my throat. My voice doesn't sound like mine. I had no idea all these thoughts were prowling around inside my head, and a part of me is ashamed they're roaring out, clawed and fanged. But another part of me just doesn't care if my words tear skin.

Alice looks at me for a long time, waiting. But I've already said too much.

Finally, she says, "Yes, I have a big house. And I wander around it alone, feeling scared all the time. Scared that my parents will forget about me, or that maybe they already have. Scared that I don't have any real friends."

I roll my eyes. "Oh, come on. You know everyone."

"That's not the same as having friends." She stares hard

at the bathroom tile. "I worry that if anyone got to know me, the *real* me, they wouldn't like what they see. And when I start dwelling on that, the worry snowballs into fear, which snowballs into panic. Sometimes it gets so bad I have trouble breathing. Like there's a physical knot in my chest, or a brick of acid, and a little more oozes out with every breath. It makes me feel like there's something wrong with me."

Like there's something wrong with me.

I'm thunderstruck. Which should technically be lightning-struck, but no matter. I can't grasp all the words Alice is saying—but on some deep, true level, I understand her.

She exhales.

"Last year, after my ông nội died, I started seeing a doctor. That's when I learned what I was feeling had a name. *Anxiety.* What a hideous word. My doctor suggested we try medication, and that helped. When I started going to a therapy group with other girls, that helped, too."

Alice sweeps the hair out of her eyes.

"I do comedy because it's the best way I've found to keep the anxiety at bay. When people laugh at my jokes, the knot of dread in my chest starts to loosen. The acid dissolves. I can breathe again. I feel . . ." She exhales. "Normal."

My heart beats all over my body. Alice is being brave and honest and vulnerable. In other words, she's being Alice.

I want to be brave and honest and vulnerable back.

But I've forgotten how to be those things, if I ever knew. All I can do is sit here silently like a piece of wilting lettuce.

I can tell there's more Alice wants to say. But her phone rings.

She checks the screen.

"Sorry, I should take this. It's my dad. He's been freaking out all day about what's happening at the hospital—patients are getting out of bed and strolling outside, even ones who are terminally ill. They think they're fine, because they don't feel any . . . Dad? Hello?"

He speaks sharply in Vietnamese. Alice's eyes go wide.

Her face twists into an unfamiliar shape.

She drops the phone, hands shaking.

"My mom's in labor, Zia. But she didn't feel any pain from the contractions and it's happening too fast."

"Does that mean she's—"

Alice doesn't hear me. She's already gone.

⊙

When I was a little girl, Mom told me a story. Thousands of years ago, a little gold star sparkled at the heart of the galaxy. "The Milky Way?" I asked, because we were learning about astronomy at school. "Even better," Mom said. "The Marshmallowy Way."

The star lived happily with her mother, a comet who was always zipping around the cosmos, and a host of twinkly friends from neighboring galaxies. Her friends loved the little gold star because she always shared her sparkle, so they twinkled a little brighter whenever she was nearby.

But as the years passed, the star began to dim. She was drifting farther and farther from her mom and friends. Galaxies are always growing and expanding, which means they are also moving away from each other.

The little gold star refused to lose them. She screwed up her starry eyes and peered deep into the universe—and only then did she see what she had missed. She was not the only one growing dim. Her friends had faded almost to extinction; her mother was a dark, silent streak in the sky. They were all being pulled, one by one, toward a ravenous black hole.

"So the little gold star did something courageous," Mom said. "She summoned all her stardust, all her gaseous fire, and burned brighter than ever. Brighter than any star had ever burned before. She poured her golden light into the sky so that the others could find their way back to the Marshmallowy Way."

"But wait," I said. "I thought the more brightly stars burned, the faster they collapsed?"

"Not this star," Mom said. "She's still burning bright. That's just the way she is."

In this story, the star was a hero. She saved her mom and

friends, saved herself, saved the whole orderly universe.

I am not that star.

⊙

The bathroom is colder once Alice leaves. Emptier. Which is how I feel, too.

But I don't go back to the auditorium where Mom and Yiayia are waiting. I don't go back to our apartment, either. I slip quietly down the hall and out of Ryden, past the soccer fields, past Mom's and my special spot. I go to the only place I *can* go, where this whole mess started.

The Attifact.

⊙

Yiayia's house is exactly the way I remember, and also completely different.

The front door isn't locked. Mom must have forgotten amid the moving mayhem. As I step inside, the stained glass skylight paints a blue kaleidoscope on the thick Persian rug. Everything smells the same: a hint of nutmeg and old upholstery. There are holes where certain pieces of furniture used to be, the stuff that's now crammed into our apartment.

I head to the spiral staircase, toward the curved wall of photographs—and that's when I see it.

All the photographs are missing. The dazzling panoramas of Greece. The faded group shots of Yiayia's friends and relatives. The pictures of Mom from tot to teen. Even happy-little-chonk Zia has vanished. Every one of us has gone the way of my pappoúli with his smiling eyes.

I slide my glasses down my nose, squinting hard over the rims. Then I climb the stairs, running my fingers along the wall as I go, feeling for nail holes or chipped paint. There's nothing. No gummy residue from glue or tape. No sign there were ever pictures here at all.

My feet move more swiftly now. I hear them thump underneath me, carrying me up the stairs and down the long narrow corridor, my hand reaching automatically for the white string.

But it doesn't matter how fast I go. I already know what I'll find when I climb up there.

The Attifact is empty.

No old books, no bursting boxes, no glittering matáki. No precious odds or precious ends. Even the cobwebby shelves are gone. Not gone as in, Mom packed them up in the U-Haul. Gone as in, they've been scrubbed from the face of the earth.

Did I do this?

I sink to my knees. Crushed by the weight of my own sadness. I've been so unbearably sad for so unbearably long.

But I have to keep moving. Have to do something before the Shadoom consumes me.

Desperately I plunge a hand into my bag. I want to put the dictionary back and pretend none of this ever happened. I keep erasing the wrong words, or maybe the right words in the wrong way. What if something happens to Alice's mom because of me? Or to the baby?

I'm not the little gold star. I'm not a hero. Every time I've erased a word, I've thought I was helping people, but all I've done is make things worse.

The babáki nests in the curve of my palm, impossibly small. How have I used so much? It's just a pinprick now. An infinitesimal black hole.

Why did I think I could help anyone else when I can't even help myself?

A hollow sound swirls into the attic.

Two floors below me, the front door creaks open. Then creaks shut.

Footsteps. Feet glide over the Persian rug. They stop at the base of the stairs.

A visitor.

The footsteps start again. They grow louder as the visitor ascends the staircase. Slowly. Carefully. The house shifts under this new weight, straining with every step. In the long narrow corridor, the carpet gobbles the sound.

The trapdoor to the Attifact jolts open with a sharp, sudden gasp.

"Paidaki mou?"

A white cumulus poof rises into view.

"Yiayia," I say. "It's just you."

"*Just?*" She isn't smiling.

"I only meant—"

"What I tell you?" She waves a hand around the attic. "What I say of this place?"

"That I'm not allowed to—"

"I say some gifts, they are given. Some you must take."

In a flash, she's beside me. I didn't know she could still move that fast. She rips the matáki eraser from my hand.

"Yiayia, wait. You don't . . ." I clamber to my feet. "You don't know how powerful that is."

"No, paidaki mou. *You* do not know."

We lock eyes. Hers are fierce and brown, clearer than they've been since the day she arrived.

"Yiayia." I speak slowly, enunciating every syllable. "What exactly are you telling me?"

"What I am telling you is, you only just begin."

Her bony fingers close around the matáki.

"I have been erasing my whole life."

erase |i-ˈrās|
verb

1 to rub or scrape out (as written, painted, or engraved letters): *erase an error*

2 to take away, removing from existence or memory: *If you had the power to erase anything from the world, what would you take?*

I gape at my grandmother. Stunned. Trying to make sense of what she just said.

I have been erasing my whole life.

"Many tears ago," she says, "I start taking the words."

A slippery epiphany lands in my gut. My mind scrolls back through the strange things Yiayia has been muttering all week. One word in particular stands out.

Many tears ago.

So many tears, gone.

In our family, we fight many tears.

What if . . .

Is it possible?

Instinctively, I sit on the bare attic floor, pulling the C. *Scuro Dictionary: 13th Edition* onto my lap. I take a deep breath and begin turning pages. As I draw closer to the Y thumb cut, my hand slows. There are barely a dozen pages of *y* words. YAM. YAWN. YEALING.

I stop.

YEAR is gone.

Only, it's not *completely* gone. I can still see the traces of where it was, the blue fibrous residue ground into the paper.

My throat clogs. Yiayia is telling the truth. She's been erasing words, too. Or trying to. She tried to erase YEAR because she didn't want to remember all that the years had taken from her. Or maybe she wanted to erase time itself.

"Sometimes I take the small words," Yiayia says, easing herself onto the floor beside me. "The words no ones notice. But sometimes I take the big from my life."

"*You are not safe in the star,*" I murmur, remembering what Yiayia said to Mom. *All the stars on the road, too many.*

I turn to C and confirm my suspicions.

Of course she took CAR. After losing her husband in a car accident, why would she want to remember that?

But when I tilt the page, I can see the ghost of CAR. Maybe that's why a piece of the word lingered in Yiayia's mind. Enough that she still worried about Mom out on the road.

I have a new theory. To test it, I flip to B, then F, then S.

BURN.

FIRE.

STOVE.

I run my fingertips over the places where those words should be, now streaked with rubbery nubbins from the babáki. I can still feel the shape of the words indented on the page, in the same way that, after you press down very hard on your pencil, you can still feel the impressions in the paper. Even long after you've erased the words.

Maybe Yiayia just wasn't strong enough to erase the words she wanted to get rid of. Or maybe the magic works differently for her than it does for me. It must be especially strange navigating an English dictionary when it's not your native tongue.

Yiayia follows my eyes to the page. She must know what I'm thinking because she says, "I try very hard. For tears and tears, I know no other way. The life, it can be so heavy. I try to take the heavy. But I cannot always take."

And then, I understand. When I erase a word in the dictionary, it comes up cleanly, leaving no trace. For me, the idea behind the word might flicker like a light bulb for a few hours, but for everyone else, the idea ceases to exist the minute I lift my eraser from the page.

Words really are my superpower.

But for Yiayia, it's different. No matter how hard she drags the eraser over the word, the ink always leaves an echo. She can never take it away completely.

With that realization, so much snaps into place. My grandmother may be struggling with dementia, but something else is happening, too. She's been actively trying to erase the heavy words.

I feel a twinge of sadness. It must be so confusing for Yiayia. Sitting in cars. Standing in kitchens. Her brain a tangle of half-faded words and meanings, in a world where those things very much exist.

Can Yiayia still see the things she's erased, I wonder? Or are they like black smudges of empty space?

No wonder she burned herself on the stove.

"I used to be strong," Yiayia says softly. "But now you have the strong. When *you* take, you take for the world."

And I know she's right. I never felt powerful until the *C. Scuro Dictionary* came along.

"How many words have you erased, Yiayia?"

"I was careful. For tears I take only the small. I save the eraser. Until . . ."

Like a shock to the brain, I know why the babáki has been shrinking so quickly.

"Until you came to live with us. You've been erasing more."

She nods. "So much heavy here. Things I have not felt for long time. And heavy, too, now that your yiayia's brain is . . ."

She brings her hand to her forehead, squeezes her fingers tight, then explodes them outward. *Poof.*

"Now that your brain is taking things away, too," I say quietly.

A shadow passes over her face. She refuses to let it settle.

"But is better now," Yiayia says. "Now I am most happy."

I remember her hunched over the stove. Crying in the emergency room. Facing off with Mom in the kitchen about some old grudge. She doesn't seem most happy.

Yiayia takes my hand.

"It is not too late. You are strong. More strong than your yiayia. We ate the donkey, just the tail is left. There is one more shadow we can take."

She taps my chest lightly, and my heart rises to meet her fingertips.

"I see your shadows, paidaki mou. I feel this same dark. It live always inside me, no matter what I take. All the women in our family, we have this sadness. We fight many tears. Our dark little room."

My eyes fill with tears. *Real* tears. Because at last, I can see it. The thread binding Yiayia, Mom, and me together. The family heirloom no one wants.

"Sadness," I say.

It's so simple. I hold it in my mouth, feeling the weight of it. The word I've been looking for.

Sadness is the true name of the Shadoom.

And it isn't just Mom and me and Yiayia who are sad. Alice is sad. Sasha is sad. Even Thom Strong is sad, he just wears it differently. The world holds so much sadness, it's a miracle it doesn't break.

I know I shouldn't have erased the things I erased. They poked holes in the universe like an exploding star, and some of the good stuff leaked out, too. I thought getting rid of those words would make people stronger, better, *happier*. I was wrong.

But this time it's different. I've been treating the *C. Scuro Dictionary* like a little kid, trying to chase after the monsters under the bed. A kid who needs Lightning Bugs and story time and marshmallow crème.

I'm not a kid anymore.

"No more sadness," Yiayia says. "You see? We fight the sad by taking away. This is our great gift to the world. Some gifts we must take."

"If we take away the dark," I murmur, "we make the light pour in forever."

I sit up straight. This is it, then. I'll use what's left of the eraser to take sadness.

I'm ready to do this. I was *born* to do this.

"Éla," says Yiayia. "We do it now, paidaki mou. Together."

Paidaki mou. *My little child.* She hasn't called me Zioula mou in a while.

Come to think of it, she hasn't called Mom by her name, either.

"Yiayia?" Gently I squeeze her hand. "Do you remember my name?"

She doesn't answer. Just waves off my question, like it's unimportant.

Something curdles in my stomach.

All this time, I've never looked for myself in the dictionary. Now I remember how the first time I opened it there were way more z pages than there should've been. But I got so caught up in everything else that I never investigated. Never even flipped to z again.

Slowly, as if my hand is moving through honey, I reach for the last thumb cut.

Z.

I'm not there.

A cool breeze sweeps through the Attifact, rippling the pale pages. They look undeniably blank as they whiffle by.

But then I see a flash of black. A dash of electric blue.

I reach out and catch a page by its corner. Lift one golden edge until it catches the light.

And I *am* there.

Or at least, I was.

The pages are stained with eraser residue, the blue and black and white of the babáki. But the remnants are unmistakable, each one grooved into the paper.

ZIA

ZIA'S

ZIA'S KITTY MOUSEIMUS WOULD LIKE A NICE MOUSE SNACK

ZIA AND SOPHIA SHARE A SCOOP OF ICE CREAM

ZIA ERASES THE SHADOOM

I suck in my breath. There are hundreds of words, maybe thousands—definitions, synonyms, example sentences under the headword. And they're all mine.

My hand reaches out to touch them, but the pages flutter forward, halting abruptly.

ZIOULA MOU

My little Zia.

"We must take, paidaki mou!" Yiayia peers over my shoulder. "What is this?"

My grandmother's gaze flits over the page. And I know,

from the hollowness in her brown eyes, that she can't see the ghost of the Zia words.

Can she even see *me*? The real, live Zia sitting beside her in the Attifact, a place that used to hold all her odds? All her memories?

Awareness snakes through me. I search for GRANDDAUGHTER. Then DAUGHTER. Then HUSBAND.

My fingers flow quickly over the half-moon notches. But it's the same every time. Smudges of color. Echoes of words.

I can tell, from the way the pages are crimped and puckered, how hard she tried to erase us.

Now I know why the photographs vanished from the stairs and the matáki charm from my hand. Why every time I tiptoed into the attic, more family heirlooms had gone missing. At the beginning, Yiayia's magic was more powerful.

But then it stopped working. Or it stopped working dependably. Sometimes the thing disappeared, sometimes it didn't. I'm guessing the dementia only made it worse.

Things escalated. The only way Yiayia knew to fight fire was with fire. So every time it got difficult, every time she felt things she didn't want to feel, she grabbed her matáki eraser and found the corresponding word in the dictionary. Then she pressed down as hard as she could, determined to take the whole word family.

I wonder when the word family became *our* family.

Of *course* she never talked about my pappoúli. How could she, when she took him a long time ago? She took her family in Greece. She took her friends. She took Tzatziki.

She saved Mom and me, for many years, many tears—until finally she tried to take us, too.

Why? Were we too big a burden? Did we make her feel too much?

"But, Yiayia," I say quietly. "Didn't you lose the good things, too?"

"Even good things have the shadows!" Her voice has fire in it. "If you have someone you . . . someone who . . ." Frustrated, she waves a hand in front of her face. "But then you lose them. And you cannot get them back. There was no one who help me, no one to talk to. So I carry the shadows always alone. I do only thing I can do. I take them away."

The truth of those words lands with a *thwack* in my gut. That's exactly what I've been doing: taking away the shadows.

Or at least, what I thought were shadows.

My voice is so small it could fit in the palm of my hand.

"What about us, Yiayia? What about the people you love?"

She frowns. "What is this, *love?*"

I don't want to look for LOVE in the *C. Scuro Dictionary.* I already know what I'll find.

My heart sinks to my ankles. Some things I understand. Some shadows I don't want, either.

But *love*? What made Yiayia decide to take love? Did living with Mom and me bring more shadows than she'd imagined? Was it just too hard?

I wonder what she erased first: love or us.

Is there really any difference?

Because for the first time, I understand something. Love is the invisible language a family speaks. Different families use different words, but the point is they understand each other. You don't stop speaking a language when times are hard. When Mom and I eat ice cream and laugh together, that's love. When I'm sad and Mom gives me a Lightning Bug, that's *also* love. Even when Mom's cranky and I'm crouchy, that's still love.

And to get rid of it forever? To take love away completely? That's like erasing every star in the night sky without realizing you erased the sun.

"Are you ready, paidaki mou?"

I nod. I know what I have to do.

The dictionary voices no objection as my fingers skate to s.

sadness |ˈsad- nəs|
noun

    1 grief, unhappiness, sorrow

    2 when you're consumed by feeling sad: *All the women in our family, we have this sadness. Our dark little room.*

By the 1300s, *sadness* was widely understood to mean "sorrowful." But the word originally derived from Old English *saed*, "full, having had enough." By the time the word evolved into the Middle English *sad*, it took on expanded meanings, such as "serious, deep" and "real, true."

Even before the ink begins to move, I know exactly what the picture is. I recognize every corner, every shape, every shadow in that dark little room. As the hinges creak, I shut my eyes and feel the door to the Shadoom close inside my chest, sealing out every ray of light.

I open my eyes.

Yiayia's gaze finds mine. I think of the battle she's been fighting silently all these years, desperate to erase her enemies one by one. Not so different from the battle *I've* been fighting, desperate to erase the parts of the Shadoom.

I think of the parts of life my grandmother has given up. Not just the shadows, but the sunny spots. The feelings she didn't want to feel. The people she loved and didn't want to lose.

You know the saddest thing? She lost them anyway.

"For us," Yiayia says, pressing the babáki into my hand.

I pull the dictionary close, smoothing the middle crease.

This is my final chance to set things right.

This time, I won't make any mistakes.

Deep.

Real.

True.

"I love you, Yiayia. And I am so sorry you are sad."

In one swift movement, I slam the dictionary shut. I hold the babáki over the curly gold script on the book's cover.

"Wait!" Yiayia cries.

Everything has a name. Even dictionaries. So I press the last speck of the eraser into the *C. Scuro Dictionary: 13th Edition.*

And I erase it.

depression |di-ˈpre-shən|

noun

1 *astronomy*: the angular distance of a star below the horizon

2 a mental disorder marked by sadness, fear, anxiety, loneliness, emotional and sometimes physical pain, and feelings of hopelessness and despair: *My family has a history of depression—my grandmother, my mother, and me.*

3 finally: a name for that dark room

In a heartbeat, it all comes rushing back.

Fear.

Pain.

And sadness. The sadness never left.

My hands are cupping empty air. No babáki. The dictionary has ceased to exist.

"Zioula mou!"

My grandmother claps her hands over her mouth. I burst into tears. She knows my name.

"I'm sorry, Yiayia. I know you wanted to take it all away." I wipe my cheeks, but the tears keep falling. "That was what I wanted, too. I'm so tired of being afraid all the time. I wanted to stop *feeling* so many things, all the hurt and sadness. But I think . . . maybe . . . maybe we can't have the happy without the sad. Maybe that's just part of being alive."

I can't believe how quickly the words come back to me. Not just the words, but the feelings behind them. The clutch of fear in my gut. The throb in my temples. Almost like they never left.

Yiayia looks at me for a long time. I brace myself for the tongue-lashing, the torrent of furious Greek.

"Éla, Zioula mou." She wraps an arm around my shoulders. "How is it you are wiser than an old Greek relic like me?"

When she hugs me, her cheek is wet against mine.

My heart crashes out of my chest. I'm elated, heartbroken, astonished, relieved—all the things. It worked. I erased the dictionary. And in so doing, erased the erasure of everything I erased.

"Zia? Mana?"

I bolt upright. Call down through the attic floor, "Mom?"

She's running. The sound fills the house, the stairs trembling under her feet as she pounds through the corridor. The trapdoor flies open, and then she's rushing toward me, bundling me into her arms, kissing my Grizzy hair.

"I was so scared, Zia. I couldn't find you after the Jamboree. You just vanished. I thought I'd lost you. I thought . . ."

She's crying, too. She reaches out and gathers Yiayia into our messy, tearstained embrace.

"I was afraid I'd lost you both."

I wrap my arms around her waist and hold on tight. I'm so happy she's here. I'm even happy she was scared of losing me. Not that I want Mom to be afraid. But I think, sometimes, fear goes hand in hand with other feelings. The people we're most scared of losing are the ones we love the most.

"I'm here," I whisper, my mouth smushed into her collarbone. "We're both still here."

And I realize how grateful I am that that's true.

"I feel like I just woke up from a nightmare," Mom murmurs. "Even though I haven't been asleep. I started doing the strangest things that didn't make any sense. And I said awful, careless stuff to both of you, because I didn't care if it hurt you. It's almost like I . . ."

She steps back. Looks at Yiayia and me, stricken.

"Oh no. I said those hurtful things, didn't I? It wasn't a dream. And you were scared of something, Sunshine Girl. Something big. But you couldn't tell me what it was." Mom knits her brows. "I don't think that was a dream, either."

All the words I've never said are building inside me. When I see Mom's worry crease, my mind scrolls through all the reasons I shouldn't add to her stress. *Don't be a burden. She's got enough on her plate. You're the Sunshine Girl.*

And then I remember one of the things Mom said to Yiayia.

Has it ever occurred to you that maybe you shouldn't have taught me to keep everything locked up inside? To bury whatever I'm feeling?

Maybe me burying my feelings is the *last* thing Mom wants.

"There's so much I want to tell you, Mom. I've never been able to put it into words. But I want to try. I just . . . I think . . . There's one thing I need first."

"Of course." She nods very seriously. "Anything you want, Zia. Just name it."

There's a lot I'm going to need from Mom. But right now, one easy thing comes to mind.

I grin.

"Easy Peasy Mac-n-Cheesy."

Sometimes help really is that simple. You name it, and it's yours.

⊙

"Who's up for an indoor picnic?" Mom says on our way back to the apartment, arms full of takeout boxes from The Sweet Potato.

I never say no to a picnic. But Yiayia looks exhausted. Now that so many words and feelings are flooding back into my brain and body, I can only imagine how *she* must feel, since she's been erasing them a lot longer.

In my heart I know I haven't magically cured her. My grandmother is fighting bigger foes than just the dictionary. By the time we're back home, she's struggling with my name again, even though I can see in her eyes she recognizes me. I don't know how many words are going to come back to her, and how much the dementia has taken away for good.

"Tonight I sleep, paidaki mou," Yiayia says. "And tomorrow . . ."

She goes to bed without finishing the thought, so I'm left to wonder what tomorrow will hold for my grandmother. For any of us.

I know one thing: we'll face it together.

Mom spreads out a red-checkered blanket and paper towels, and since the fancy table vanished with everything else summoned by the dictionary's magic, we eat our Mac-n-Cheesy on the living room floor.

We talk. We laugh a lot, like when the Mac-n-Cheesy gets a little *too* Easy, and long tendrils of orange cheese dangle from our mouths. But Mom makes it clear tears are welcome, too.

"Tell me everything you're feeling. Even if it's confusing or hard to say. I want to hear it all, Sunshine Girl."

I can feel Mom's stress crease on my own forehead. "That's sort of the thing. I don't . . . I'm not really . . ."

I take a deep breath.

"I'm not the Sunshine Girl, Mom. I haven't felt sunny in a long time. But I don't know how to talk to you about it, because you're dealing with enough already. So I try to put on a brave face and be your sunbeam. Except for the times I get so scared and sad I just can't keep pretending. Those are the times I ask for a Lightning Bug."

"Like last night." Mom sets down her fork. "I'm so sorry I couldn't give you a Bug, Zia. I was tired and frustrated. But I shouldn't have put any of that on you. It's not your job to make me feel better."

She cups my chin.

"You are my sunbeam, and you always will be. But that's true whether you're sunny or not. You don't have to *do* or *feel* or *be* anything."

Mom drops her hand. Picks up her fork and pokes at her Mac-n-Cheesy.

"I know you get sad. I get sad, too. It's something I've struggled with my whole life. And I was so scared I'd passed it on to you. The family curse. Ever since you came back from Sasha's party, I knew something wasn't right."

Mouseimus plops down between us, offering up his furry belly. Mom gives it a nice rub.

"I'm still figuring this out," she says, "because even moms have a lot to learn. But you know what I think?"

"That Mr. Mousie likes to insert himself into serious conversations?"

She smiles. "I do think that. I also think it's better to talk about things than to not talk about them. Your yiayia always kept her feelings buttoned up inside. When I muster up enough empathy and compassion, I understand why. She'd left her country and her family and her friends behind—of *course* she was sad. Mana thought that shutting down emotionally was the only way to survive. So she taught me to do it, too. To slap on a happy face and pretend to be sunny."

Mom looks me in the eye.

"But I don't want to teach that same thing to you, Z. It hasn't worked for me. Sounds like it's been causing us both a lot of pain. I think we can do better."

I close my eyes, letting those words land inside me. What would that even look like? Dishing up all our gross, jiggly feelings like the cafeteria ladies dishing up scrod?

And then I see Alice. Crouched in the girls' restroom, sharing her deepest secret. How brave she was to tell me the truth. I've been so scared to tell anyone about the Shadoom because then they'd know I was broken. But when Alice told me about her anxiety, I didn't see someone who was broken. I saw someone who knows and loves herself for exactly who she is—and isn't afraid to ask for help.

"The Shadoom," I say simply. "That's what I call it."

The word hovers in the air between Mom and me. Hideous. Haunted.

And yet, in a way, having it outside of me—floating over the checkered blanket, ruffling the fur on Mr. Mousie's belly— is a whole lot better than having it locked up inside.

The breath rushes out of me in one long gust.

"It started the night of Sasha's party, and it's been inside my chest ever since. It's a room full of all the stuff I'm scared of, and the places that hurt but I could never reach with a Band-Aid, and then all the ways I'm sad. And it's not just me. If the people around me are sad, the Shadoom sort of sucks up their sadness, too."

Tears spring to my eyes, turning my glasses into two misty circles. The Shadoom is hard to talk about. But I don't stop.

"I've been trying so hard to act like I'm okay. I make up words and funny ship names because I love making people laugh. I'm the little gold star who can make everyone bright and happy. But all I can see inside me is that dark shadowy room."

I stare down at my Mac-n-Cheesy. The macaroni has congealed into a lumpy orange sea.

"I didn't know what to call it. And you know me. I don't have trouble coming up with words! That might be the worst thing. Not only was I dealing with the room all by myself—I couldn't name it, which only made it worse."

Mom's gaze is steady. No sympathy sounds, no telling me it'll all go away. Just her full, undivided attention.

She tucks a strand of Grizzy hair behind my ear.

"I know exactly what you mean, Zia. It's called depression. At least that's the best name I've found for my Shadoom."

Depression.

I chew on the word. It's a kind of whisper. A hush.

"Depression," I say, trying it on for size. "It sounds so soft."

"It does, doesn't it? Talk about a word that does not feel the way it sounds!" She cocks her head. "Want to look it up in the dictionary?"

"NO!" I shout.

"Okay! Sheesh!" She holds up her hands. "We'll just google it instead."

"Yes. Good." I nod vigorously. "Google is good."

Mom goes to get her laptop, which gives me time to revive my heart until it starts beating again. I understand the laptop dictionary is no C. *Scuro.* But something tells me I might be steering clear of all dictionaries for a while.

Together, from our cozy nook on the living room floor, Mom and I google *depression*. The first result is some kind of clinic for mayonnaise, followed by a bunch of serious, vaguely scary-sounding websites.

"Well, *this* looks depressing," Mom jokes. "Let's try *depression in kids*."

Those results are better. Colorful charts and lists of signs and symptoms. Mom toggles to an image search, and every single picture is of a kid curled into a cashew shape, usually with their back against a wall. Look, I've got nothing against cashews. I know that shape well. It's just funny to imagine you have to cashew yourself against a wall to be depressed.

When Mom starts reading snippets from some of the articles, I can't believe it. A lot of kids and parents have their own names for the feeling when it comes. The Gray Guy. Blue Days. One Canadian kid named Mark calls it Dark Mark.

I'm flabbergasted. Other people have the Shadoom, too. They just call it different things.

"Do you know what a comorbidity is?" Mom asks, and I shake my head. "It's when someone experiences two illnesses at the same time. They get kind of . . . intertwined. This says one of the most common comorbidities for depression is anxiety."

I perk up immediately—and not just because *comorbidity* is an amazing word. I now have one more reason I get Alice, and Alice gets me.

Then I wince, remembering my harsh words in the girls' restroom.

I hope I haven't royally messed things up with my friend.

"Look at this," Mom says, clicking on a link. "It's a local therapy group for girls your age. Something called Self Collage."

I remember what Alice said about going to a therapy group with other girls. Curious, I peek over Mom's shoulder.

"How do you collage your Self?"

"Looks like you cut out pictures and make collages to express what you're feeling, then share with the other girls in the group."

Mom sets the laptop aside.

"Here's something to think about, Z. I want us both to feel like we can talk honestly about what we're feeling. But not everyone will be a safe space for all of our messy, goopy, glorious feelings. So it's a funny balance we're trying to strike, you know? We want to be brave about sharing our truth, while also being wise about who we choose to share it with. Not everyone deserves your whole heart."

I nod. Just because I want to tell Alice I'm depressed doesn't mean I want to shout it at the top of my lungs to the entire Ryden cafeteria.

"Do you think the other girls at Self Collage will be a safe space?" I ask.

"Maybe. I hope so. But only you can decide. And if it isn't a good fit, then you make like a banana and split."

I ruminate. What would it be like to cut out pictures with other girls while we talk about our feelings? I've never done anything like it. I've always thought of myself as more of a word nerd, less a pic chick. But I have to admit, I'm intrigued.

"I'm a logical person," I say, pleased at my turn of phrase, because the root of *logical* is *logos*, the Greek word that means "word." "But maybe I could try being Collagical for a while."

Mom throws her head back and laughs.

"There she is! My wordy girl." She plants a kiss on my forehead. "I think Self Collage is a terrific idea. And if you don't like it, we'll find something else."

I feel my forehead pucker, the worry creeping back. I readjust my glasses.

"But won't it cost money?"

"Oh, Zia." She touches my cheek. "I'm so sorry you've had to worry about that. It hasn't always been easy, I know. But if there's one thing I know about us, it's that we will figure it out. We always do."

She snugs an arm around my shoulders and pulls me close.

"I'm your mom. I will always find a way to take care of you and give you all the Lightning Bugs you need. I should never have dumped on you about money and work stuff. I promise to do better." She pauses. "I think it's time I find a therapist myself."

Mouseimus steps smugly onto our Mom-Zia pile, until we

are one glorious heap of Mousemomia. I feel warm and fuzzy on the inside, too.

Something Yiayia said comes back to me, about always having to carry the shadows alone.

Poor Yiayia. She didn't have someone to talk to when she was hurting. I'm so grateful I do.

Mom scratches Mr. Mousie under his furry chin.

"I love this little kitty. And I love my girl to the stars and back."

I nestle my face into her neck. It's not like the Shadoom is completely gone, but it feels different. Lighter.

My chest is full of Lightning Bugs, dancing in the dark.

☉

That night I call Alice. I want to tell her everything, but I'm also scared of what she'll say. Last time we talked I was awful. And then she got the call from her dad.

The phone rings for so long I don't think Alice is going to pick up. Which leaves plenty of time for me to imagine all the worst-case scenarios. If the whole world went back to pre-dictionary normal, surely that means Dr. Phan Number One and the baby are okay, right?

Alice picks up.

"Hey, Zia."

"Hi! Howdy!" Apparently I revert to cowgirl when nervous.

There's a long, heavy silence. In it I hear all the cruel things I said to her. I want to tell her I'm sorry, but I don't even know where to begin.

I take a breath.

"Listen, Alice . . ."

An intercom blares in the background. I realize she's still at the hospital.

"Is your mom okay? How's the baby?"

"She's fine. They're both fine."

The relief wallops me so forcefully I have to sit down.

"I can't tell you how happy I am to hear that."

Alice pauses. "I have a little sister."

"That's amazing! What's her name?"

"Lily Hope Phan. My parents let me choose her middle name."

"That's perfect, Alice." I'm beaming. "See? You've been a big sister now for, what, an hour? Two hours? And you're already the world's greatest."

I hear her shift, like she's trying to get comfortable in a scooped-butt chair.

"I told my parents everything," she says finally. "About Story Club and how I want to be a stand-up comic."

"What'd they say?"

"They already knew. I guess my math tutor ratted me out." She sighs. "They weren't mad about Story Club. They were mad I'd lied about it. But mostly they were sorry. They apologized for being so focused on the new baby and said they never want me to feel like I'm being pushed aside. It was really sweet. They also said they wouldn't ground me for lying about Story Club . . . if I could make them laugh before my mom's next contraction."

I kind of love the Phans. "And did you?"

"No." She takes a beat. "I made them *cry*, they were laughing so hard."

My heart glows in my chest. I'm so happy she can finally share the thing she loves.

"You're so good with words, Alice. I know you think I am, too. But the things I've been feeling this year . . . I haven't known how to talk about them. You were brave and honest enough to share what you've been going through. And I couldn't hear it."

I gulp some excruciating air.

"I want to be brave and honest with you, too. You've been a safe space for me from the start. Actually, you inspired me. I'm joining a therapy group next week."

"That's great, Zia."

But her voice is stretched tight. I can't tell if she's angry or hurt.

"Alice, I'm so sorry. I was mean to you for no reason."

More silence.

"You didn't deserve the stuff I said. I want to make it up to you, if you'll let me."

Double scoop of silence.

Then she says, "You're invited to my birthday party next weekend."

It's such an abrupt change of subject, I can't think what to say.

"I know it's last minute," she goes on. "I didn't think my parents would let me throw a party, because they'd be too preoccupied with Lily. But they said twelve is a big deal, and we should celebrate. So if you want to come . . ."

I close my eyes. I can see it so clearly: Sasha's backyard. My last attempt at a birthday party.

My eyes fly open.

"Of course I want to come," I say, because I don't want to be afraid of parties anymore. Or birthdays. Or peach cobbler.

"Your mom and grandma are invited, too." Alice's voice sounds less tight. "I'm actually pretty excited. My parents said I could put on my own backyard jamboree."

My tongue shrivels in my mouth. "A Story Jamboree?"

"You don't have to tell a story," she says quickly.

"No, no, I figured."

Make that a triple scoop of silence. I am dying a thousand deaths.

"Alice, I'm really—"

"I have to go," she says, her voice tight again. "See you at school."

collage |kə-ˈläzh|
noun

ɪ a creative work that incorporates various elements: *Joy makes beautiful collages.*

verb

ɪ to collect different things and arrange them into something greater than the sum of their parts: *I'm not so shabby at collaging myself.*

"Thanks for joining us, Zia. Welcome."

It's my first day in the Self Collage group. I'm so nervous I keep forgetting to breathe.

But Joy—crackerjack name for a therapist—is the kindest human on the planet. She has a heart-shaped face and curly dark hair, and she's brought chocolate-covered cashews for us all. I get a little tickled, imagining a bowl of tiny depressed kids dipped in chocolate.

"Welcome, Zia," the other girls echo.

Joy leads us in a round of introductions. There's Emily with rainbow hair, Diya in a zebra-striped tank top, and Skip, who's been coming here the longest. I don't know Skip or Emily—they go to a different school, and anyway, they're seventh graders—but I've seen Diya at Ryden. She's on the soccer team with Jay and has a belly laugh that's bigger than she is.

At first I'm embarrassed. Will Diya think there's something wrong with me for being here?

Then it hits me: She's here, too. We're in this together.

"Pick whatever images you're drawn to." Joy gestures toward stacks and stacks of pictures she's cut from glossy magazines. "They could be happy or sad. We don't always know *why* we're drawn to an image. That's okay. One thing I've learned from doing this work is that sometimes our souls know more than our conscious minds. Choose the images that speak to your soul."

Joy shows us a card she made with a sea turtle swimming in a deep blue ocean. She's glued smaller images around it— baby turtles, dolphins, and a woman dancing with her arms lifted. The card gives me a whipped-butter feeling in my chest. It's wild and peaceful at the same time.

"Do I use scissors to cut the pictures so they fit on the card?" It's a weirdly specific question, bbut I've never collaged anything before, and I don't want to get it wrong.

"There's no wrong way to do it," Joy says, making me wonder if therapists are psychic. "Personally, I prefer to rip them by hand. I like my images imperfect, a little rough around the edges. They seem more real to me that way."

I get the feeling she isn't only talking about sea turtles.

"Can we play some music?" Skip asks. "I made a new mix."

Joy nods, and as an elegant piano melody fills the room, we begin.

⊙

For the next half hour, I tell the wordy part of my brain to pipe down so the images can speak to my soul.

And here's the thing.

I *love* it.

Some images I'm drawn to make perfect sense, while others surprise me. A purple night sky sprinkled with stars. Boats in a harbor. A piece of toast. There's even one picture of a dark room with shabby torn curtains and a crooked door hanging from one hinge. Looking at it makes my throat clench. But Joy said to choose the images that speak to us, and sometimes sadness speaks loudest of all.

Ultimately I wind up with a starry night above the dark room—and a fat tabby cat sitting on the roof eating a marshmallow.

"Before we share our cards with one another," Joy says, "I'd like to offer you a special phrase that can help unlock the wisdom of the images. *I am the one who.* It's almost like you're letting the images speak to you, *through* you."

I'm having a hard time understanding this, so I'm glad when Skip volunteers to go first.

She plunges right in. She tells us how she's really been missing her grandparents. "I used to bake with my gran every Sunday. While the cookies were in the oven, my papa would teach me how to fix old clocks. I loved my time with them. But I just couldn't spend one more hour hearing them call me the wrong name. They haven't *once* called me Skip. They won't even try! To them, I'm a he. But I've always been a she."

She lets out a slow breath, then tucks a shock of hair behind her ear.

"Every time I get triggered, I just remember what my mom tells me: 'You're not the one who's wrong, Skip. *They're* the ones who are wrong.' It doesn't make the ache go away, but it helps."

I'm blown away by how easily Skip talks about her feelings. I'm even more blown away by her collage, which is good enough to be in a fancy museum. She's pasted together dozens of images: shimmering butterflies, strands of golden lights, tall majestic sequoia trees.

She stares at her collage a long time before she speaks.

"*I am the one who is lovely,*" Skip says. "*I am the one who is quiet but strong. I am the one who has always been here.*"

And that's how the conversation moves around the table, from one person to the next.

"*I am the one who embraces my stripes,*" says Diya. Her card is covered in zebras galloping under a raincloud. "*I am the one running under a dark cloud. I am the one who is depressed.*"

Hold the phone. Diya is depressed? When I see her at lunch, she's always smiling. Not to mention that huge belly laugh. I never would have guessed she was anything but happy.

Next up, Emily cries when she tells us her parents are getting divorced. Her card only has one image: a house she tore in half so there's a jagged space between. But as she repeats *I am the one who*, she seems to find comfort.

"*I am the one who is afraid of losing my home. I am the one who feels torn between two places. I am the one who loves both my parents—and deep down I know both my parents love me."*

I can tell how much better Emily feels when she's done.

"Zia?" Joy says. "Are you ready?"

"I think so." I want my card to reveal new truths to me, too. After all: words are my jam.

I stare down at the collage, opening my mouth so the images can speak to me, *through* me.

And suddenly all I can see is the dark room.

The long shadows.

The broken door.

I take off my glasses, rubbing furiously at my eyes. I really don't want to cry in front of four strangers. Even though Emily did. Even though I know by the looks on their faces that no one would judge me one bit.

I clear my throat and force out the words.

"I am the one who is scared of the dark."

"I am the one who is broken."

"I am the one who is alone."

My heart feels like a burnt marshmallow plooping off a stick.

What happens when you *do* find the words, and they don't make things better?

"Thank you for sharing yourself with us so bravely, Zia," Joy says softly. "This work isn't easy. It can dig up a lot of emotions, and you're being very courageous to go to those places, even when it's hard. Would it be helpful to hear what the rest of us see in your card?"

I nod, though I can't imagine how that would help.

Diya eagerly slides my card across the table. "Ooh! I have a kitty exactly like this! Your kitty is eating a marshmallow, which means he has excellent taste. And at first it seems like he's alone, but actually, I don't think he is. See those shapes right there?"

She points to something I hadn't noticed in the corner of the card. "There's a whole family of squirrels in that tree."

I stare in amazement. Those *are* squirrels, or at least the silhouettes of squirrels. I was so focused on Mr. Mousie's alter ego I couldn't see them.

"Okay, and see how the door is hanging off its hinges?" Emily says, pointing. "It casts a really pretty shadow on the wall, almost like the sail of a ship. If the door weren't broken, there wouldn't be a ship."

She slides the card over to Skip, who studies it for a moment, then smiles.

"I see a gorgeous starry night," she says. "The moon is full, and the stars are so bright they're shining into that dark room. And—go with me here—the holes in the curtains let in the moonlight. If they were, like, perfect whole curtains, they'd block out all the light."

I can't describe what I feel, listening to the others talk about my card. They see so many things I missed. They see the good amid the bad. The beautiful amid the broken.

"Can I go again?" I ask, and Joy gently sets the card back in front of me.

"I am the one who is afraid."

"I am the one who is fearless."

"I am the one who is broken."

"I am the one who is strong."

"I am the one who is not alone."

When I'm done, I look up at Joy to see her eyes sparkling.

"Have you ever heard of chiaroscuro, Zia? In Italian, *chiaro* means 'light' and *scuro* means 'dark.' It's a technique artists use to contrast light and shadow. If your whole card were as bright as those stars, you wouldn't be able to see anything at all. Our eyes are drawn to the light *because* of the dark. They're both important."

"It's true," Diya says. "My mom's a painter, and she says behind every light you can always find a shadow. And behind every shadow, you can always find a light. *Chiaroscuro*. It also sounds like a girl's name, though I've never actually met a Chiara Scuro, have you?"

Wait a minute. Chiara Scuro.

C. Scuro.

The *C. Scuro Dictionary.*

The tingles start at the base of my neck.

A book full of shadows is also a book full of light.

"If we never felt sad," Joy says, "then we'd never feel happy. A world without sadness wouldn't be much of a world, would it?"

A smile tugs at the corners of my mouth.

"I can't even imagine."

birthday party | ˈbərth-dā ˈpär-tē|

noun

    1 a party thrown in honor of someone's birthday

    2 the perfect excuse to eat copious amounts of

dessert: *Why not serve chè trôi nước at a birthday party, the*

best dessert in the whole history of desserts?

Alice's birthday party is quite the production. Literally. Her parents rent a temporary stage for the backyard, and her Story Club teacher is the MC. Alice invites all her guests to tell a story, play music, or do anything they like. Then she headlines with her new set.

She's brilliant, obviously. Funny, honest, real. I'm so proud of my friend.

The problem is, I'm not sure she's still my friend. We've hardly said more than *hey, hi* at school all week. And she's been avoiding me since I got here. It's her party, she's busy, I get it. But I can't shake the feeling that I didn't apologize right. Watching Alice onstage, my heart keeps rising in delight, then sinking in despair, bobbing up and down in my chest like a duck.

I don't like ducks.

Luckily, there's plenty to distract me. I can't believe all the people who showed up for Alice's party. To my surprise, Thom is here, looking uncomfortable in a bow tie. He astonishes everyone when he pulls out a viola—and plays the most gorgeous, haunting song I've ever heard. Guess his musical tastes extend beyond heavy metal.

I see his mom milling about the other adults. She looks different than she did in the ER. Her bruises are gone, as is

Thom's cast. I heard a rumor that Thom's parents split up, and for both his mom's sake and his, I hope it's true.

The memories of that strange, whirling week seem to have faded for everyone, even Mom.

Except for me, of course. I remember everything. It's a little bit lonely.

Luis brings Snape onstage, and they're both totally hamming it up, or maybe *mouse*ing it up, since Luis feeds Snape a frozen pinkie mouse. The lump moves slowly down his body, inch by inch. Everyone is freaking out.

I actually think it's cool. Maybe I'll ask Dr. Lopez if she needs a herpetology assistant. I wouldn't mind being amphibextrous myself.

When I see Sasha stride onto the stage, my mouth goes dry. I still haven't been able to talk to Sasha and Jay. I'm too scared of what they'll say. For a fleeting moment, I consider hiding inside Alice's house—my go-to trick at parties, apparently—but I force myself to stay put.

"So I wrote and directed a mini-musical," Sasha informs the audience. "It's a new art form I made up. Keep in mind we're still workshopping it. Real artists are always workshopping."

Jay shuffles nervously onto the stage. But since her character is supposed to be nervous, it works. She's playing the part of Shelbie, an aspiring singer who always chokes at auditions but is amazing when she sings in her dreams. Of course Shelbie is wildly talented, so her dream self composes and records a whole musical while she's asleep. Turns out the video was real—she really did record a whole musical—so naturally it goes viral.

Meta, you might say.

Sasha plays Shelbie's dream self, her voice as jaw-dropping as ever. I scan the audience, taking note of all the jaws that have dropped.

After the last note of the last song fades, they get a standing ovation. The audience goes wild. I'm so giddily proud of Jay and Sasha, so in awe of their talent, I find myself walking toward them once they've fended off their fans. I have no idea what to say—and I don't even care.

"You guys," I say, breathless. "That was incredible. You totally nailed your monologue, Jay. And I knew you could sing, Sash . . . but I had no idea you could write and direct, too."

"Isn't she amazing?" Jay gushes. "*So* brilliant. When she gave me the script, I was like, how is this so good?! I just feel like you should be on Broadway, Sash. Don't wait till you're eighteen. You should be on Broadway *now*. Watch out, world! Did I mention that Sasha Davis is—"

"*Jay*," Sasha and I laugh in perfect unison.

The three of us stare at one another. Startled. It's been a long time since we were all on the same page.

And then, in exquisite harmony—we burst into

simultaneous giggles. The exact kind of simulgiggles that made Zashay special.

"You guys!" Jay wipes her eyes. "Cut me some slack, okay? I'm working on it."

I didn't know how much I missed them until this very moment.

Sasha turns to me.

"I'm glad you enjoyed it, Zia. We weren't sure . . ." She and Jay exchange glances. "We didn't think you liked us anymore."

"Wait, what? Why would you think that?"

"We've spent months trying to guess why you ran out of my birthday party. We didn't know if it was something we said or did."

"No! It wasn't that at all." I gape at them. "Have you really thought that all this time?"

And it dawns on me. How that night must have looked from Sasha and Jay's point of view. Me leaving without telling them, whisked away by Mr. Davis under cover of darkness. Then avoiding them at school.

Sasha and Jay don't hate me. They thought *I* hated *them*.

"I am so sorry," I say, with every ounce of sorry in my heart. "I promise I'll explain everything. I should have done that a long time ago. I just . . . couldn't."

Jay smiles. She itches a mosquito bite on her elbow, then loops her arm through mine.

"We've missed you, Z. We really have. No one's ship names are as good as yours. *No one's.*"

"Do we need to stage another Complimention?" Sasha says, but as she loops her arm through my free one, she's smiling, too.

We stand there for a second, all linked up. Basking in the familiar comfort. The joy.

Zashay.

When we finally unlink ourselves, Sasha clears her throat.

"Maybe we could have a sleepover next weekend? We could, you know. Talk about stuff."

I picture Sasha's house, pool, backyard. For some reason, it doesn't seem quite so scary now that our feelings are on the table.

"Under one condition," I say. I think I'm ready to take the plunge.

"What's that?"

"Peach cobbler. Bowls and bowls of peach cobbler."

Sasha laughs. "I'll put in a request."

My glasses are fogging up again. I take them off, ready to buff the yellow suns. But they don't need it. They're already shining.

I glimpse Alice standing a stone's throw away. She's slurping down a sticky rice ball, trying not to eavesdrop. But her anxiety is written all over her face.

I know that look. She's afraid we're going to leave her behind now that we've made up with each other. My heart goes full-on duck again, because while I don't want Alice to be scared, it means she cares. The word *scare* is really just *care* with an *s* tacked on the front.

I turn back to Sasha. "Hey, can Alice come to the sleepover, too?"

"Of course." Sash grins. "I've been trying to get her to come over for ages."

"Now that her mom's had the baby," Jay offers, "I'm sure she'll say yes."

My heart droops a little. I'm not so sure.

Sure enough, no sooner has Alice swallowed the rice ball than she darts away from us, disappearing into the crowd.

"I'll catch up with you two later," I say to my friends.

"Parting is such sweet sorrow," Jay intones, sweeping a dramatic hand across her brow.

Sasha clutches her heart. "Until we meet again."

☉

While I'm looking for Alice, I spy Mom. She's standing apart from the other adults. Hugging the food table, nibbling cheese cubes and pretending she isn't nervous.

She really is the grown-up version of me.

I'm glad she came. Last week she found a home health

aide to come to our house so Yiayia wouldn't have to stay alone. Mom is also talking to Yiayia's doctors about elder care facilities. Some words and memories have come back for my grandmother, but others haven't. It hurts to see her struggling to remember my name. Especially when I can see it hurts her, too.

But we're all doing the best we can. We are getting better at finding light between the shadows. Laughter inside the sad.

As I watch Mom eating bottomless cheese cubes, Dr. Phan Number One appears beside her, a tiny Lily Hope swaddled to her back. She pulls Mom toward a small group of people, and they open the circle so she can join. Soon they're all smiling and bobbing their heads the way adults do.

A bearded man with light brown skin and a friendly smile leans in a little closer when Mom talks, laughing at all her jokes. Which is weird because—no offense, Mom—her jokes aren't *that* funny.

I feel Mom's eyes searching for me in the horde of kids. When they land on me, she relaxes. Whatever happens next, we're going to be okay.

"Zia!"

It's Alice, her face flushed.

Hope surges in my chest. She's talking to me.

"I just saw you signed up to tell a story!" she says.

She's not wrong. I figure I've got to give this storytelling thing one more go, even if I'm terrified. And I am definitely terrified. But it's the good kind of terror. The kind that makes my toes go numb and my chest go fizzy.

"Listen, Zia." She holds my gaze. "I'm sorry I've been distant."

I shake my head vehemently. "No, no, no. Alice, *I'm* sorry. This is my fault, not yours. I feel awful that I was mean to you. You didn't deserve it."

"It's true. I didn't." She folds her arms over her chest. "I won't lie. It hurt, the things you said."

I nod miserably. "I know."

"But I appreciate your apology. I know you were going through a lot. I just needed a little time to sit with it."

"I hate that I hurt you. I don't know if I can forgive myself."

"Well, that's up to you." Alice unfolds her arms. "But *I* forgive you. So there's that."

She smiles, and my heart-duck sprouts wings.

"On that note," Alice says, "I want to give you something."

"It's your birthday. Aren't I supposed to give *you* something?"

I'm super excited about Alice's birthday gift. Mom talked to one of her ladies at the dance studio who runs a comedy club, and they agreed to waive the "eighteen and up" policy to let Alice perform one night.

"Whatever it is, I'm sure I'll love it," she says. "But first."

Alice takes my hand. I feel a heady rush.

"A surprise."

Alice |ˈa-ləs|

noun

    1 a popular female given name

    2 a hilarious twelve-year-old girl who can tell a joke like nobody's business: *Alice is going to be a famous comedian someday.*

    3 my friend

Alice leads me to a little private alcove in her backyard—away from the other partygoers, but close enough to hear the MC announce the next act.

"You're up soon," Alice says, snapping the hair bands around her wrist. "So I better make this quick."

"I really am curious about those bracelets." I know the MC will call my name any minute, but my curiosity wins out. "Even if I was a total jerk about it before. Why *do* you wear them?"

"I was wondering when you'd ask."

She's quiet for a moment. The only sound is the gentle pop of elastic against skin.

"It's something my therapist suggested. I snap the gray one when I feel scared. It gives me courage. The red one is for when someone hurts my feelings, or for like when I stub my toe. Makes the pain more manageable, you know?"

"And the violet?"

Her smile has a story buried inside it. "That color always makes me sad. The morning my granddad died, my mom burned a bunch of lavender. I remember sitting there, breathing in the smell of lavender and holding my ông's hand until his skin got cold."

A lump climbs up my throat. I've only just begun to build a real relationship with my yiayia. How long before I lose her?

"But that's so sad," I say. "Why would you want to remember it?"

"Why would I want to forget? Ông Nội was like my second dad. I was glad I got to be with him at the end. I cried and cried, but I cried because I loved him so much. We're supposed to feel sad when we lose the people we love. That's what makes us human."

I want to tell Alice I've been thinking the same thing. How, in my new therapy group, we get to talk about the stuff that hurts—and the stuff that makes us human. We don't *change* those feelings. But we use them to create something beautiful and real.

I want to tell her that I still get sad and scared, but knowing other kids also get sad and scared . . . it helps. That's why I'm about to walk onto that stage and share a little of my story. I feel like, once I started talking about my depression, the people in my life rose up to meet me.

I readjust my glasses.

"Do you remember how that day in the girls' restroom, you asked me what I wanted?"

"You said you wanted to get rid of the Shadoom."

I nod, pleased she remembers. "I think what I really wanted was to not be broken. I was sure there was something wrong with me."

"Broken?"

Alice laughs. It streams into my ears like pure sunshine.

"You're the wholest person I've ever met. You're strange and honest and hilarious and true. Every time we talk I feel like my heart glows a little brighter."

My own heart feels like it might spill over. It's fuller than it's ever been, jam-packed with everything—sadness, joy, fear, pain, depression, hope, love. But it's a big heart, bigger than I ever used to think it was. Big enough to hold all those things without breaking.

My heart is my heart. And now, finally, someone else sees it . . . and likes me anyway.

No. She likes me *because* of it.

I reach out and gently pluck the gray hair band on her wrist, then the red, then the violet.

"These don't help you forget," I say, finally understanding. "They help you remember."

She nods. "Precisely."

"You amaze me, Alice Phan." I shake my head in wonder. "I might have to get myself some of these."

"Actually . . ." She reaches into her back pocket. "That's the surprise."

When her hand reemerges, three brightly colored elastic bands are nestled in her palm.

Brown with black stripes.

Pale peach.

And electric blue.

"I tried to pick Zia colors," she says, pinching the brown-and-black band with her free hand. "I know how much you love your tabby cat, and this seemed tabby-colored."

She pokes at the peach. "You get a little . . . how do I put this . . . *strange* when people talk about peaches? That seemed important. Peach clearly makes you feel things. And then this . . ."

Alice loops the blue band around her index finger, twirling it in a perfect circle.

"This one just felt right to me. Blue is such a sad color. But it's a beautiful color, too."

I'm having a hard time forming words. Not a feeling I'm accustomed to. How did she know these were exactly the right colors? I couldn't have chosen them better myself.

As my gaze rests on each band, I let the memories rush in. Scratching Mr. Mousie's tabby tummy, gripped by fear. Peaches and pools and a dagger of bright, hot pain. The dark blue of the deep end and the outer ring of Yiayia's matáki charms. All the days when the blue just won't come out in the wash, no matter how hard you scrub.

"I wanted you to have these," Alice says. "Consider it a gift from A to Z."

She lays the three rings flat on my palm. Her fingers linger an extra beat.

"That way, no matter what happens, you'll remember that fear and pain and sadness are a part of living. Even if sometimes you wish you could erase them."

Her sharp eyes lock on to mine.

A chill sweeps down my spine.

Even when everyone else lost the things I erased . . . even after I did . . . Alice held on to them. She still spoke the words. Still felt the feelings.

I gasp.

Alice knew about the dictionary. She *always* knew. And she still remembers.

I open my mouth to speak, when—

"Zia Angelis!" the MC announces. He's onstage, ready to hand over the mic so I can tell my story.

My whole body is tingling. I stand and slip the hair bands over my wrist. Alice's eyes twinkle. There's a matching twinkle in mine.

"I have so much I want to ask you, Alice. So much! But I guess I'll just have to wait."

Alice grins. A dash of magic and a dollop of mischief.

"Go knock their socks off, Z."

⊙

This time, I know all the words.

A NOTE ON ZIA ERASES THE WORLD

I was eleven years old when I faced my first major depression. The Shadoom seized me without warning, and my world went dark. Much like Zia, I thought there was something seriously wrong with me. It took me many years to understand that mental illness is simply another kind of illness. Just like bodies get sick, so do brains. Depression is a biological, medical condition—and it *can* get better if you treat it with the right tools.

Everyone's mental health tool kit looks a little different. Alice has anxiety, and her treatment involves therapy and medication (which may not be right for everyone). Zia takes a huge first step by talking to her mom about the Shadoom. She also joins an art therapy group led by a licensed therapist. I believe therapy can be powerful, both individually and in a group setting; it gave me great comfort at eleven and continues to enrich my life to this day. Zia's Self Collage session was inspired by my experience with SoulCollage®, an expressive arts practice that has been profoundly healing on my own journey with depression. If you'd like to learn more about SoulCollage®, I've included a link in the resources below.

Maybe you, too, struggle with fear, pain, or sadness. Or maybe you feel overwhelmed in a different way than the characters in this book. No matter what you are going through, please know this: *There is nothing wrong with you.* Mental illness is not your fault. Right now your brain may be whispering that you are completely alone. You're not. Like Zia and Alice, lots of kids struggle with their feelings. The first step is to talk to a trusted adult or mentor, someone who makes you feel safe and supported. That might be a parent. It might be a grandparent, aunt, uncle, friend's parent, teacher, librarian, guidance counselor, or coach. If it's easier to express yourself through written words or images, go for it. You could even point to a line in this book that feels true to you.

Here's the good news: once you have that conversation, your tool kit has already started to expand. Your trusted adult can now reach out to trained professionals and access a variety of mental health services. On that note, I've included some resources below that I've found helpful. I hope they shine a little light into the dark.

National Alliance on Mental Illness

nami.org/Your-Journey/Kids-Teens-and-Young-Adults/Kids

Anxiety & Depression Association of America

adaa.org/find-help/by-demographics/children/anxiety-and-depression

Child Mind Institute

childmind.org/topics/depression-mood-disorders

Mental Health Literacy

mentalhealthliteracy.org

Crisis Text Line

crisistextline.org

This Is My Brave

thisismybrave.org

SoulCollage®

soulcollage.com

ACKNOWLEDGMENTS

By now you know weirdlings are tiny weirdos. But do you know what *wordlings* are? No? Well then. I give you, with tremendous pleasure, the last surviving entry of the *C. Scuro Dictionary*:

wordlings |ˈwərd-liŋz|
plural noun

1 the unique constellation of talented, tireless, and wonderfully wordy humans without whom this book would not have come to be.

2 House of Random Penguins in Viking helmets: the best wordlings in the biz.

a. Maggie Rosenthal, the chiaro in the chiaroscuro: You have poured so much light onto this journey for me. Zia glows more brightly because of you.

b. Kelley Brady and Opal Roengchai: words cannot express how beautiful you made this book—and I have words for everything!

c. Dion MBD: You designed a cover that set my soul on fire. You're the dreamiest kind of sorcerer.

d. Sola Akinlana, Krista Ahlberg, Abigail Powers, Esther Reisberg, and Madeline Newquist: Your clever notes filled my nerdy wordy heart with joy. I face-plant (hyphenate) at your majesty!

e. Kaitlin Kneafsey, empress of publicity, and all mages of marketing: I am abundantly grateful for your skill and tenacity in ushering Zia onto the world stage.

f. Ken Wright, chief wizard of wordlings: thank you for saying yes.

3 Readers and agents and brains (oh my!): the wordlings making magic behind the curtain.

a. Kimberly, Miranda, Gwen, and Victoria: Your thoughtful, incisive reads didn't just make this book better—they made me better. All shortcomings are my own.

b. Nandini Ahuja: The work you do is vital. Thank you for helping my readers feel seen.

c. Brianne Johnson, who said the magic words ("Write the book you needed at age eleven"), and Allie Levick, who wore every hat with panache: thank you for helping me grow Zia into the girl she was always meant to be.

d. Andrea Somberg: Your enthusiasm for this book means the world. Here's to many more.

4 Masters of middle grade: genius wordlings crafting their own wordthings.

a. Katherine Applegate, Tae Keller, Rebecca Stead, Marie Cruz, and Corey Ann Haydu, whose books made me weep, laugh, and remember: Thank you for showing me what is possible. I am beyond lucky to have your words gracing mine.

5 Rock stars of the next generation: this book sparkles all the brighter for the brilliant young wordlings who read it.

a. Cam, Brianne, Sean, Jenna, Shelbie, Kathleen, and Wyatt: thank you for being star players in my Story Jamboree.

i. (And kudos to Dana, Jacqui, Tamara, Paula, and Rebecca for loaning me such stellar interns.)

b. Holly Lash and her Wolverines: Your notes came exactly when I needed them. I <3 you.

6 Friends of the heart: I might need to stage a Complimention, because all I want is to bombard you wordlings with nonstop compliments to a degree that's almost worrisome!

a. Alison Cherry, Cori Nelson, Dana Davis, Honora Talbott, and Teresa Spencer: You kept the faith, even when I lost the thread. Thank you for bravely sharing your own experiences of depression, anxiety, and apologizing to inanimate objects.

    b. For all my Sassy Djerassis: Where would I be if you hadn't read those early pages?

    i. Shellie Faught packed love into every margin note;

    ii. TJ Ohler's kilarious messages kept me going;

    iii. Nova Ren Suma: Your support has buoyed me more than you know. What Alice says to Zia at the end is almost verbatim what you once said to me. I had to preserve it in print!

7 Teachers, therapists, pastors: the gentle souls who guide little lost wordlings like me.

    a. Joy Malek, Donna Peddy, Mrs. Jenny Liu: I am here because of you. My heart is full.

    b. Steve Stark: You comforted me when the doctors couldn't. Thank you for seeing me.

8 Wordling family: Like a word family, only better, because you're mine.

    a. Cat, the true Sunshine Girl: You believed in this book from the beginning. You are my sunbeam, and you always will be. But that's true whether you're sunny or not.

    b. Christopher DeWan, who read more drafts of this book than anyone, and sat beside me many times in that dark room: You are my favorite wordling AND my favorite weirdling. Our life together feels like coming home.

    c. Mom: When I remember those first days of the Shadoom, my most vivid memory is of crawling into your lap in the soft blue rocking chair. You always made space for me; you never ran out of Lightning Bugs. There is a reason Zia's mom is her hero: you have always been mine.